# COLOUR COMES TO TANGLES

By
## JONI SCOTT

To Marion, for all the haircuts, lovely chats and
years of friendship.

# ABOUT THE AUTHOR

Joni Scott has enjoyed a scientific career as an organic chemist and biochemist in hospitals and industry. She also home-schooled her two children and then embarked on another career running a tutoring business. After writing her debut novel, *Whispers through Time*, she contracted CRPS and lost the use of her dominant right arm and hand. In early 2020, she travelled to Italy for treatment but ended up in lockdown. This experience inspired her second novel, *The Last Hotel* which she wrote with her left hand. Though the physical act of writing is still a struggle, Joni continues to write in a strange tippy-tap manner. *Time Heal my Heart* will be released soon as her fourth novel and can be read as a free-standing novel or sequel to *Whispers Through Time.*

*Colour comes to Tangles* is Joni's third novel and is a contemporary mystery romance, partly set in India.

Joni also co-hosts a women's encouragement blog where she writes articles about women in history and today. Read the blog at **whisperingencouragement.com** or connect with Joni via her website at **joniscottauthor.com** or on Instagram under **@authorjoniscott.**

# PROLOGUE

## Burnt Orange, the colour of flames

### Surat, North India, 2015

Flames lit the night sky. Smoke followed, billowing from the ground floor of the large stone building, then soon after, from the second floor as well. Cotton is very flammable.

The town of Surat depended on the fluffy white bolls harvested in nearby fields. Now they burned along with the looms and vats of colourful dye, destroying the income of a whole community.

For almost a century, The Chatterjee Cotton Factory had been its life blood. Local men, women and girls worked in the production, gathering and transport of cotton as well as in the factory itself. Using traditional skills, they wove and dyed the plant product into colourful clothing and homeware, mostly for the export market.

But it seemed someone did not have the same pride in the success of the Chattergee factory. Did they watch hidden by the darkness of night as flames engulfed the factory? Did they return later to view the smoking charred skeleton of the massive building? More importantly did they realise workers slept in the adjoining residence at the rear of the site? For the police determined the fire as arson and possible murder. Chatterjee workers died that night whilst they slept. The manager, Vinni Patel was unable to save his wife and brother-in-law.

# CHAPTER ONE

## The Rainbow

### Buderim Mountain, Queensland, Three years later

My Josie went missing the same day I met Vidisha. These two women did not know each other. Their only common link was me. It was one of those life coincidences of time and place like the week when your toaster, microwave and computer all stop working together. Stargazer Amy had even forecast as much that morning in her weekly horoscope column, confidently predicting that for all Aries, 'Appearances and disappearances will be important this week.'

Josie is my friend, one of my two best friends. Bubbles is the other. For ten years, we have been a close trio. I met Josie and Bubbles at my hair salon. It is mostly how I meet everyone, even how I met Vidisha. Newly immigrated and fresh from India, colourful Vidisha came to live and work in Buderim, right above my salon.

Everyone wants to live in Buderim, the higher up the mountain, the better, because the views are amazing. From any side of the top of Buderim Mountain, you can see forever, north to Noosa, South to Caloundra and Brisbane beyond, east to the blue Pacific and west to the Blackall Mountain range.

Originally, locals called only the actual mountain top, Buderim, but later developers of the mountainsides fashioned names such as North Buderim or Buderim Meadows to capitalise on the prestigious name. The mountain itself is a volcanic outcrop plateau in Queensland, Australia, originally forested with stands of magnificent red cedar.

But the British colonialists came, and timber getters exploited the natural forests. Once cleared of its valuable timber, the area became a settlement of farms. The rich volcanic soil was perfect for agriculture. In the late 19th century, the locally grown Burnett Coffee won awards in London. Later ginger farms flourished in the area and Buderim Ginger became famous world-wide.

In this prime position, on the top on the mountain plateau near the centre of the township, is Wisteria Park. The park is a grand old darling of a park, a precious reminder of the days of gracious homesteads and gentler times. The massive, century old Weeping Fig trees survived as their beautiful spreading branches deliver welcome summer shade, a filtered light filled space for modern residents. Their compressed leaf fall forms a soft carpet on the shaded ground beneath them, offering a perfect and magical place for children to play.

The fig trees once stood guard along the entrance to the pioneer family homestead, Wisteria. The home is sadly long gone, given over to modern residential development, shops, and roads. Directly across the road from the park is a row of shops, an old corner store, a bakery, an antique store and my hair salon.

This salon in Buderim has been the focus of my existence for the last twenty years. Hairdressing is my work and social life all rolled into one and this airy large salon, my second home. Is there time or inclination for socialisation after talking to clients all day, six days a week? Definitely not.

So, there have been few surprises in my routine life until Vidisha came and until I met Vidisha, I didn't appreciate how dull my life really was.

When I arrived for work, on that Monday, the day Josie went missing, I noticed a new sign on the outside wall of the building. With my keys poised, about to unlock the latches, I read it.

***Vidisha Patel, Psychologist and Chromopath*** it said in a lovely flourish of gold lettering. To my surprise, next to the writing was a small painted rainbow. The symbol of the rainbow had in recent years represented the LGBTQ population in all its diversity, so I assumed this 'person' who had set up practice above my salon was of this persuasion. That did not trouble me at all as I had friends and clients who identified with the rainbow.

Demi and Dale who owned the corner store two doors down were good friends and an all-girl couple. Really, any tenant would be more pleasant than the previous one, a grumpy unfriendly lawyer of indeterminate middle age who invariably wore a crumpled grey suit. Few clients had climbed the stairs to consult him in his five years of tenancy. Rumours spread of his bankruptcy.

Reappraising the sign, I wondered if Vidisha was a female name. One never knew with foreign names. Patel, surely though was of Indian origin? The name was familiar from the credits of Bollywood movies. I eagerly awaited meeting this new upstairs tenant with the lovely name and rainbow.

After opening my salon, I carried my 'No Appointments Necessary' sign out onto the pavement outside. My thoughts of the new arrival vanished as I gazed over at the leafy park.

Was that Sean, again? A slim dark-haired man sat on a bench in the park, his face shaded by the trees. Sean had sat there before, watching me from a distance. The large windows of the salon allowed such an activity, such 'stalking,' if one wished to label it so. Josie had urged me to view these sneaky predatory visits as such.

'Just march over Tan, and tell him to bugger off!' she encouraged.

Josie was like that, very forthright. She was getting even more outspoken as she 'aged.' Not that Josie was old yet, but just mature, fifty-four to be exact, five years older than me.

As I set up trays of utensils and bottles of bleach and colour for my 'cut and streak' client, due soon, I sensed the figure in the park move. Once he was out from the shade of the large Ficus fig tree, I knew it was Sean. My stomach churned, my heartbeat quickened. They were here again, those familiar sensations I was helpless to control.

Then, to my alarm, Sean crossed the busy road at the pedestrian crossing and appeared soon after, right outside my shop. How dare he! My heart thumped relentlessly and the familiar clenching in my stomach gripped me in its vice. *Please just leave me alone. Go away, Sean.*

But he didn't. Instead, he pressed his face to the window. Separated by the glass window, we stood looking at each other, The name of my salon, TANGLES, painted in large blue letters across the window, partly obscured Sean. But his face stared back, curiously circled by the centre of the large loopy letter 'G' of the TANGLES.

His eyes met mine. I always felt weak and wobbly when confronted by those large, brown 'puppy dog' eyes. This time, panic added to my discomfort. Glancing at the clock, I noted that in five minutes Glenda would be here for her appointment. She could even be earlier. Glenda was always punctual, especially for a 9 am time slot. Rushing to the door, I decisively yanked it open so the bell above it tinkled loudly in protest.

'I came to see you, love,' Sean said softly, coming towards me, outside the shop. His eyes appealed to my kinder nature. He was aware of his effect upon me.

'Well, you've seen me! I have a client coming. You must go, Sean!' I snapped, surprising myself with my vehemence. Josie would be proud.

'Can we have coffee? I want to talk to you.' he pleaded.

'We are talking, and no, we can't have coffee. I am working, remember. I work, like most people. You should try it sometime,' I exclaimed.

I avoided his eyes, instead hurling the words sideways at the passing traffic. If I looked into those deep brown pools fringed with incredibly long lashes, (how dare a male have such lashes) I would soften and I must not soften, be kind or let him into my life again. He must go.

Yes, he had to go because my client, Glenda, all smiles, walked towards me after crossing at the lights. Glenda would be eagerly anticipating our chat and the welcoming coffee from my newly purchased Nespresso machine.

'You have to go, Sean! Now!' I hissed at him. Turning, I entered the salon, leaving the door open for Glenda, only Glenda.

'How are you, Glenda?' I greeted with forced gaiety. 'Come sit over here, dear.'

Glenda eased her bulk towards the chair and sat with a resounding sigh.

'Well, I've had a bit of trouble with my knee and Bill is off at the doctors again. It's his sugar diabetes you know.'

Yes, I did know. Glenda always talked incessantly of her latest health dramas, or more aptly, 'lack of health' dramas. Sugar diabetes for heaven's sake, who called it that, these days? It was diabetes type 2, thank you. And if Bill lost weight, reduced that disgusting over-hang of a pot belly, he wouldn't have the blessed 'sugar' diabetes anyhow. Visits by Bill to the salon, certainly proved that he had not slimmed down over the past years.

Today with Sean lurking, I wished Josie or Bubbles were here, not boring Glenda. I needed distraction, not the same boring domestic and medical details Glenda would share for the next hour and a half. But embracing activity, I set to work, mixing the peroxide, powdering the streaking cap. There was no need to ask Glenda what she wanted today, because that was a done deal.

Glenda always had the same, every six weeks to the day, a trim and streaks to maintain her 'Princess Di' hairdo. Princess Diana's beautiful face and signature hairstyle had graced many magazines in my salon for years until her tragic and premature death in 1997. Her blonde bob hairstyle had been popular, a common request, 'I want to look like Princess Di.'

'Ha-ha, don't we all?' I always replied.

Certainly, over the years, I had tried my best to transform hair of all types and shades into the famous bob, Glenda's hair being no exception. Most women changed their styles, colours, even hairdressers, but not Glenda. Even though Diana's bob was no longer the rage, Glenda was loyal and steadfast. Glenda was always the same; plain, overweight, and dull. As I pulled the strands of Glenda's hair through the tiny pores of the plastic streaking cap, tightly positioned on her head, I snuck furtive glances towards the park.

'Ouch!' shrieked Glenda.

'Oh, I'm sorry, Glenda!'

*Concentrate, Tanya. Don't let Sean get to you.* I told myself.

*Was Sean still there? Had he skulked off elsewhere? Maybe for a coffee and pie at the bakery two shops down?*

'Ouch! You're hurting me, Tanya.'

'Sorry, Glenda.'

'You are off your game today, Tanya. What's wrong?'

'Oh, it's nothing really. Just family issues.'

'Anything to do with the fellow that was here when I came?'

'Yes, sort of. He's my ex and a bit of trouble.'

'Pity. He's a handsome fellow,' Glenda replied.

It seemed a good time to leave and pour a coffee for us. I didn't want to tell Glenda about my private life though she was most happy to tell me about hers. In between sips of my coffee, I lathered purple peroxide mix onto Glenda's head. Soon her hair lay flat and smothered in purple goo. I wrapped the confection in plastic cap and left Glenda to 'marinate.'

With perfect timing, customer number two entered. The bell over the door announced the arrival of Barb for a haircut. I liked Barb. Barb was easy to talk to, friendly and actually interesting. As Barb prattled on about her life and work in the next-door dental surgery above the shops, I found myself forgetting Sean opposite. I had seen him sitting enjoying his pie and coffee during Glenda's-goo application.

Robotically, I finished the cut, farewelled Barb and returned to rinse the goo from Glenda. I blow-dried her blonde bob enjoying the warm air blast for it was quite cool in the salon today, being mid-August.

Apart from a gobble of my cold toasted sandwich, mid-afternoon, I kept going, attending to clients all day until 4.30 pm. I then swept the strands of variegated hair from the floor, rinsed the basins, and put the towels in my take home laundry bag. As I hauled the sign in from outside the salon, I scanned the park out of habit.

Sean had gone, sometime between the perm and the toddler haircut. He didn't like it in the park once the school kids came after three o'clock. Sean had never wanted kids. I had at first but after the money troubles set in, I changed my mind. Sean was unreliable, invariably unemployed, always in debt. I didn't want that for a kid, I didn't want that for myself. Therein lay the trouble.

ၐ

At home that night I consulted the meaning of the word 'chromopath' that had accompanied Vidisha Patel's name on the wall. The word 'chromopath' was unfamiliar. Mr Google informed me with his usual breakneck speed that a chromopath was a colour therapist. *How interesting! Therapy using colour, how does that work?*

ၐ

I had only to wait until the next morning to discover the answer to this question. For when I arrived at work, there, by the salon entrance and under the new sign, was a small perspex box filled with colourful brochures. *Oh, I'll have one of those, thank you.* Pocketing one in my cardigan, I let myself into my premises.

'I'll read you later when I have a chance,' I told the brochure. While preparing for my customers, a flash of colour caught my attention. Outside, an attractive woman in an orange pant suit with a turquoise sash paused then entered the staircase well next door. *Ah! Could this very colourful person be the new tenant Vidisha? Only time would tell.*

But despite this welcome happening, this break in the sameness of my life, I totally forgot about her then as my mobile rang and it was Max, Josie's husband. I knew his voice immediately. Max has an impressive, mellifluous voice with an attractive European accent. Max is Czech.

'Have you seen Josie?' he asked without any preamble. Straight to the point. That's Max. Always eager to sell you something. A box of amazing vitamins, a bottle of new beaut cleaner, once even some silky lingerie.

'Get in now, Tanya and you will benefit from the flow on effect. Now is the time to establish a solid base for your business.' This was the usual Max spiel.

It was hard to keep up with his current business obsession as Max's business 'opportunities' came and went in rapid succession. Each time Max excitedly told me of the latest one, which was 'the one.' And each time I assured Max I already had a business, thank you very much.

But Max would just scoff, 'That's not a business, Tanya. That's a prison. It's slavery. You need freedom, a passive income that just keeps giving. Build from the ground up with good people and you will be set for life. You'll never have to work again.'

Max has a one-track mind, and it is not the usual track most men are on. Max is on the money track. Despite having inherited a small fortune from his well-off Jewish parents, Max wanted more. He 'invested' to build a bigger fortune. But his investments were not wise like his father's. Gullible because of his love of money, he rushed in with the wrong people into the wrong businesses. He'd take a risk and lose big time over and over again.

I had heard it all from Josie. Max did not learn from his mistakes. Because he never acknowledged them. Instead, he worshiped at the altar of Multi-Level Marketing Companies, one after another. He also dabbled in supposedly lucrative insurance schemes and negatively geared real estate purchases that inevitably went wrong. Max constantly stirred many pots, all with poor yields. After twenty years Max was 'broke' and getting more desperate.

'Well have you seen Josie, Tanya?' Max reiterated. His polished voice disrupted my reflections. He sounded impatient. For once, he had not uttered the words 'opportunity' or 'business'.

'Um, no, I've been working all day, here at the salon.'

As the words left my lips, I realised with an inner groan that Max would be contemptuous of such a confession. He scorned work, real work, where you use muscles and move. His idea of work was sitting at a computer sending emails or ringing people, exhorting them to join his company, 'Dream the dream,' was his mantra, along with 'Think big, earn big.' He referred to himself as an entrepreneur, a facilitator of fortunes. I'd seen his glossy business cards.

'Well, she didn't come home last night. Where can she be?' Max asked.

Shocked, I replied, 'Really? Wherever can she be?'

'Well, that's why I am ringing you. You're her friend, you should know.'

I could have retorted with 'You're her husband you should know' but it was no time for wise cracks. My friend went missing overnight. Where was she?

# CHAPTER TWO

# My heart feels ice blue

## Where is Josie?

I promised Max that I would ring around and get back to him. And that is exactly what I did. Fortunately, it was the end of the day and there were no more clients. I sat on the pink floral sofa by the window that functioned as my waiting room and scrolled through my phone contacts. Bubbles was my first call. She, like me, had just finished work, so answered from her car. I told her Josie was missing. Maybe the fact she worked at an aquarium elicited her first reaction.

'That sounds fishy,' she said. 'No, hun, I haven't seen nor heard from her since last week at Elixibar, when I last saw you all,' she added. 'I can't recall her telling me she was going anywhere special.'

'Okay, Bubs,' I said and rung off. I needed to ring around, so couldn't waste time chatting.

Max had already rung Hen, Josie's sister, so I concentrated on other contacts. Each time though I received a similar answer. 'No, we haven't seen Josie. She didn't say she was going anywhere, sorry, Tanya, can't help.' For the third time,

I rang Josie's daughter, Tasha, but again there was only the voice mail. Max had already tried contacting his children.

Despite the impression that all young people live on their phones I had noted they never answered them. Phones to them were tools for social media, quick payments, and photos, rarely used as actual phones. How strange the world was becoming. No wonder we are mortal. If we live too long the ever-changing world becomes an alien place.

Shrugging off these philosophical thoughts on the way of the world, I rose to make myself a coffee. As I looked out onto the street, the woman from upstairs left the building in a flash of arresting colour. Now I had a closer view of her side on, I noted she was beautiful and possibly Indian. Her long straight black hair flowed down her back contrasting wonderfully with the orange pantsuit and turquoise sash that accentuated her slim figure. Her arrival in our shopping strip certainly added a much-appreciated touch of the exotic. Then I had an idea who might know where Josie was. Of course!

Demi and Dale might know. They were the owners of The Corner Store next to the pie shop on the downhill side of my salon. If anyone knew it would be them. They had their finger on the pulse of local life and Josie was a regular at their shop because she lived nearby, only a few streets away. So regular that she ordered a tea or coffee every day there and enjoyed it while sitting in the tea garden at the side of the store. Lorraine, Demi's mum would often join her for chat.

The Old Corner Store, true to its name, was old, dating back to 1900 when it functioned as the general store. The distressed green weatherboard building, positioned so its fly-screened entrance faced the main road, had seen a lot in its day- the patriotism and flag waving when The Great

War broke out, the sad news about Gallipoli then jubilant headlines as the war ended. The store had sold the newspapers that told these stories of life as it unfolded. Later, between the wars, the headlines had shrieked the news of The Great Depression, The Wall Street Crash and again another war after the one that had boasted to be 'the war to end all wars.'

Now in the 21st century, the digital age threatened the newspaper business. But Demi and Dale still stocked newspapers for the older residents of Buderim. Demi and Dale liked the 'old fashioned' way of doing things, despite, being new age women.

By the time Demi became the new proud owner, she already knew the store and everything about it. As a child, she had helped after school, usually staying till tea-time, 6.30pm, when her father, Frank, first closed the screen, then wood outer door and flipped the OPEN sign to CLOSED. The family would then retire to their flat above where Demi now lived with her partner, Dale and mother, Lorraine.

Demi had abandoned her publishing career to take over from her father. She could not bear to see the store close its doors or be fashioned into a groovy coffee shop or fashion boutique. She had already seen so many other local landmarks, like churches, halls and corner shops be remodelled, fit for modern purpose. Developers demolished some to make way for apartment buildings. No, Demi decided her dad's store would not succumb to progress, to tourism as long as she was around to stop it. It would stay and maintain its original function as a handy, well-stocked bastion of Buderim Mountain. Never mind if it was a curiosity now, with its peeling paint, old windows, and striped awning.

I hurriedly approached the old shop, three stores down. The store was long and narrow as it extended deep into the corner block and opened into the street behind where original houses now operated as doctor and dental surgeries. Above the store was a three-bedroom flat where Demi and Dale occupied one bedroom and Lorraine another. From those east-facing windows you could see the distant ocean off Alexandra Headland near Mooloolaba.

On a fine day, small yachts dotted the azure blue Pacific and further out, the outlines of passing cargo ships defined the horizon. Loaded with huge containers, they headed north from Brisbane to South-East Asia and ports like Port Moresby, Jakarta, and Singapore. Today, I did not pause to admire the view.

I, like Josie, am a regular visitor to the store. Before I had my own Nespresso machine in situ, this was my 'go to' place for coffee. Demi would often bring me an unsolicited free coffee and stay for a brief chat.

Customers to her store often confused the two D's. Perhaps it was the fact that both women had four letter names starting with' D' or maybe it was their appearance. Both Demi and Dale were slim, wiry girls with short cropped brown hair. But I knew the difference within a week of their arrival as managers. With an eye for detail, I noted early on, that Demi wore lots of beaded bracelets on her right wrist.

'They're home-made, you know. I make them myself,' she'd told me. 'I love beads and Mum taught me how to thread them as a girl. I've made them for friends and family, even sold them at the local beach-side markets.'

'I like them Demi,' I'd said. 'They're great. You could make necklaces, hair ties too, maybe.'

'I'll make you a batch, Tanya,' she offered. 'I will even make a big batch and you can sell them at your salon, you know as an add-on. Sort of like Macca's. Would you like fries with that? You could offer a bangle with a haircut. Hey, I just had an idea! Tangles with Bangles!'

I smiled now at the memory of the bangles and touched my wrist. The brightly coloured beads tinkled beneath my fingers. Now past five thirty, the store lights were on. Closing time was just an hour away. There were a few customers grabbing last minute groceries for their evening meal. I had done the same often. Though a little more expensive than the supermarkets, the store was convenient and friendly. They didn't call them convenience stores for nothing. As I entered, a middle-aged customer clutching a risotto packet and block of cheese, validated this by proclaiming, 'So much handier and friendlier than Woolworth's.'

The store inside was even more curious than its jaded exterior. Demi and Dale had discussed the interior when they took over after Frank's funeral. Demi's mother, Lorraine retired from involvement and passed the running of the shop to 'the girls' as she called them.'I worked here 40 years, Dem. It's all yours now. Your dad would be happy about you carrying on the store.'

The inside charm surprised many customers. On entering, they would exclaim, 'Wow! My Goodness! Oh my Gosh!' or the equivalent. Then, once inside, they would either complete the purchase as quickly as possible in order to escape the 'musty old store,' or fascinated, linger a little longer. As their eyes took in the ancient cash register, the lolly jars and wicker baskets of produce next to the milk shake machine, they realised they were in a time-warp. Though the lay-out was different to Frank's era, the counters were the same.

The store could be classified as part museum. Memorabilia from years gone by featured on shelves along with essentials such as cornflakes and canned soup. There were original Arnott's biscuit tins in red and gold, meat grinders, flour bins and milk churns along with metal balance scales from the times when groceries were sold by weight not in packets.

Many a customer had joked, 'You should charge admission, girls. It's a veritable museum.' Demi and Dale would smile. They loved their store like their similarly minded nostalgia fans. As I entered the store that evening, Demi greeted me.

'Tan! How are you, darl? Working late today?'

'Well, no, not really. I stayed back to make a few calls. Max rang to say Josie is missing. She didn't return home last night. Have you seen her today?'

'Oh my gosh! Heavens, no, I haven't noticed her today. I'll ask Mum and Dale. They're in the back. Come through.'

I followed Demi as she weaved her way from the brightly lit front section of the shop to the storerooms. Dale was unloading some packets from a big box and Lorraine was stamping prices on them. I greeted my friends.

'Hi Dale, Lorraine,'

'Tanya ! How are you dear?' asked Lorraine looking up. Dale flashed me a weary smile.

'Well, I'm a bit worried. Josie is missing. Max rang to say she was away overnight. He doesn't know where she is.'

'Oh, my. That is strange. Young Josie is always so dependable,' commented Lorraine.

I smiled at the reference to Josie as 'young'. But I suppose Lorraine viewed anyone twenty years her junior as 'young'.

'I didn't serve her tea or coffee today, did you, Mum, Dale?'

'No.'

'Nor me.'

Josie had not been here today.

Ice clutched my heart. Where was Josie?

# CHAPTER THREE

# Pink Champagne, lemon wedges and cherries on the top

**One week earlier**

'Cheers, Chin Chin, Bottoms up!' Three women clinked glasses in a sign of solidarity and declaration of friendship. We were not celebrating anything, just life.

'Your usual poison looks a trifle more decorative, Josie. Are you trying a different potion?' asked Bubbles.

'No, it's still Cinzano and lemonade. It just has a lemon wedge, and a swizzle stick for some reason and a cherry,' answered Josie. 'Maybe there's a new bar man?' She looked over at our glasses. 'I see you guys have your usuals. Bit harder to jazz them up. But those frosted glasses are a nice touch!'

Bubbles had her signature pink champagne, and I sipped a white wine, always a Sauvignon Blanc since it had become fashionable. Tonight, was our girl's night out, one of the many 'every second Fridays', a fixture on the calendar for ten years or more now since we had all met through my salon.

Tonight, we gathered at a new venue, the Elixabar, a slightly more up-market option than the local beach-front surf clubs. The food would be more interesting here, we had decided, a change from the chicken schnitzels and mixed grill fare of the clubs. The lighting also was more kind considering Bubbles and I were approaching fifty and Josie was a trifle over that milestone. Elixabar was a stained-glass enthusiast's paradise in the centre of the town. The overhead light fixtures were colourful hemispheres of variegated grass that sent whirls of colour around the pale green walls.

'The crowd here will be a bit more up market and younger,' I commented. We shared a smile. Yes, it was a change from the clientele of the clubs which attracted the baby boomer set and family groups, particularly on Tuesday nights when the menu featured the seniors' specials.

'Don't be too ageist, Tan. We are probably the oldest ones here,' replied Josie. Because her friends were younger, she often was aware of her age and tonight was such an occasion. The young couple at the neighbouring booth looked as if they were on a first date. They had only eyes for each other. Had they even looked at the menu yet? Josie had already spent a few minutes perusing the menu when she arrived before me and Bubbles.

'What are we having? There are some great sounding tapas plates, or we could share a grazing board?' she asked.

'Let's have both. I'm famished. Think I forgot lunch somehow,' chirped Bubbles.

I reflected that my cold toasty also seemed a distant memory.

As if he had read our thoughts from across the bar, the young waiter arrived to take our order. On asking, he replied, 'Yes, I totally recommend the swordfish in wasabi and the mozzarella bites, and the grazing board is a diner's delight to share.'

We put in the order and relaxed again with our drinks.

'So, how's the whole Sean thing going, Tan? Has he been around again?' Bubbles asked.

'Yes, sure has, most days this week. I'm getting a bit sick of it. It is annoying to arrive at work and find he's there in the park. Then he comes over and peers through the 'g spot' at me.'

'The 'g spot'? Whatever do you mean?' the other two asked in unison.

'Well, you know, the 'g' of the Tangles sign. He peers through it a bit like Sammy the Seal at Under Water World. You know how you see Sammy's little seal face through the porthole of the pirate ship? Well, it's the same because Sean has brown doggy or rather sealy eyes like Sammy, especially designed to appeal to the heart, make you soften. Sammy just wants a fish, but Sean, well, you know what he wants,' I explained.

'And he's not getting it. Don't give in again, Tan. Last time it cost you $30,000, because of his spending, remember? Who else but Sean goes out and spends thousands on stereos and speakers and those game boy toys when they have no income?' Josie reminded me. She was not a fan of men spending money unwisely because of her experience with husband Max.

'Yeah, I know. I'm a sucker for Sean. Always was, since we met at high school.'

'And he's still the same lazy, hopeless Sean,' Josie said with vehemence. She knew the ways of such men and leapt to support me. Max gambled behind the guise of 'marketing opportunities.' Like me, Josie realised too late into the marriage that such opportunities were just opportunities to be fleeced of your money.

'Sean's back on Centrelink benefits, and once he's on the hand-out he'll make no effort. I know the only time he made one was when we were first married. He was briefly productive like I was briefly beautiful. You know, the long blonde hair, heavily mascaraed days. Thank God we didn't have kids. How could I have managed, working all these years?' I remonstrated.' Yeah kids are hard work especially when you need to juggle work, but you are still beautiful Tan. You have a great figure and gorgeous eyes. Don't put yourself down,' Bubbles maintained.

Bubbles spoke from experience. She and Brad's Brady Bunch of five had kept them on their toes, for sure. Brad worked two jobs; one, underground mining, the other plumbing and Bubbles did the bookkeeping for both as well as working in a pet aquarium store.

'Oh, you will be able to blow bubble kisses to the fish,' we had teased when she first started at Aqua Tropicana, some years before. But really, Josie and I were in awe of her energy, Brad's too. He told people jokingly that he was - a minor plumber or a plumb miner or just plumb crazy. During the child rearing years, Brad and Bubbles had barely seen each other. He left at 5 am and returned after 7pm.

The lion's share of the child-rearing fell to Bubbles by default. Lunches were like an assembly line of plastic boxes and drink bottles. School pick-ups she could do in her sleep. She had been a mum-robot for years.

'You two were lucky, you escaped all the school stuff, you know, the lunches, pick-up, drop-off, homework,' Bubbles proclaimed.

She included Josie as Josie had home-schooled her two children. God knows why you would want to keep your kids with you 24/7, but Josie had, maintaining it was easier that way. Mind you, Josie was smart. If anyone could home-school, Josie could. She managed all that maths and science, plus Josie was a very patient person. She rarely lost her cool with the children but had been known to throw a saucepan or two at that maddening husband of hers.

Many a woman would have done the same or worse if theirs had lost money hand over fist like Josie's Max. From Amway through to Herbalife, Max had tried to stack vitamin pyramids to his benefit with little thought to the consequences of failure. Max's exploits were a much-discussed topic along with Sean at these girl's night get togethers. Brad passed inspection so was left alone.

The meal arrived, interrupting their conversation. It looked and smelt marvellous.

'Mm, heavenly. So much better than Chicken Schnitz. I love it when someone else cooks!' purred Bubbles.

The others concurred, raised their glasses to toast each other and tucked into the share platters, transferring portions to their own smaller plates.

'Foreign food tastes great, hey. Sure, beats sausages and mash, any day,' Bubbles exclaimed.

'Yes, thank God for multiculturalism. Best thing that ever happened to this place. The meals of my childhood were too tragic. Lamb chops, sausages and horror of horrors, steak and kidney! I remember the first time I tasted Spaghetti Bolognese. I couldn't believe how good it tasted,' Josie extolled.

'Mine was kebabs with heaps of hummus and tabbouli back in the eighties,' chirped in Bubbles. 'What about you Tan? What was your first multi-cultural experience?' she asked.

'Oh. Probably something Asian. Yes, it would have been Thai or Indian, for sure. And I still love Thai because it's so fresh and healthy. You know me, love my veggies.'

'Well, plenty here. This Greek salad is amazing and the Mozzarella Bites divine. This Lamb Sizzle's great too.' Josie enthused.

By now the young couple at the adjoining table were eating as well so with conversation at a minimum, the background music became more noticeable above the scraping sound of knives and forks. It was a chilled song playing, one we recognised as Al Stewart's 'Year of the Cat.'

Bubbles hummed along in between mouthfuls. She was a pretty woman, young looking for her nearly fifty years with crinkled long tresses that gleamed golden in the light of the restaurant. Her real name was Belinda, but no-one ever called her that. Even her toddler grandchild called her Nanny Bubbles. It suited her so. Bubbles, by name, Bubbles by nature.

She had great dress sense so always looked marvellous. Bohemian dresses with jean jackets and Doc Martin boots, like champagne, completed her signature style. Tonight, she wore a lacy white gypsy blouse with an ankle length floral skirt that flirted along the top of her Doc's. However, despite her airy name tag, Bubbles was a woman of substance, every bit capable of managing business accounts for Brad and coping with the huge demands of raising five children. Two were her own and the other three, Brad's, a collection of children, a Brady Bunch assembled from their previous marriages.

Josie had two children, a teenage boy, Aiden and a daughter, Tasha, from her marriage to self-titled businessman, Max. I had saved myself the trouble due to the trouble with managing Sean, the man-baby.

It was not really that surprising that we three women were all blonde-haired. The sun and surf environment in sub-tropical Queensland bleached even mid brown hair to a blondish shade. Josie had the wildest hair, thick and at times as unmanageable as straw. She refused to wear it short, that would be giving into her tyrant of a mother who always berated Josie about her hair. I supported Josie in this matter.

'You have great hair and plenty of it, Josie. It just needs moisturising and often', I would say, daubing great dollops of conditioner on Josie's scalp at shampoo time. Then I would cut and layer Josie's mop, finishing with some leave-in hair tonic. Josie would look reasonably tame for a few days before the frizz set in once more, doubling the volume of her blonde mane. Josie complemented her wild appearance with a hippy dress style of flowing colourful skirts and dresses. You never saw Josie in jeans because she owned not one pair.

'I'm not a pantser. Only dresses for me. I feel panicky in trousers, all fenced in. I don't know how people can wear jeans in this weather. If I get hot, I can always stick a leg out in the breeze but in pants, you are trapped,' Josie had explained.

We had nodded in understanding. Each to his own, we thought.

My style is difficult to type. I wear whatever, always something practical though. Black T shirts and shorts for the salon and mostly khaki shorts and non-descript T shirts for the garden and shops. But I can surprise. I occasionally don a dress.

'Wow, Tan, did you buy a dress?' friends would comment.

'No, just some old thing I had in the back of my cupboard,' I would reply.

Meal eaten, the conversation returned to its previous intensity. We huddled a little closer as the swelling numbers in the dining area made it harder to hear each other.

'What are you up to tomorrow, girls?' asked Bubbles.

'The usual, for me, just the salon,' I answered.

'I have a few students in the morning then the usual relaxing recreation, maybe a dog walk, some baking. But Sunday, Hen and I are going to see Mum,' announced Josie.

'Oh, good luck there, old girl,' we said, laughing.

We knew all about Josie's mum who lived in a local nursing home. We had even been treated to the irascible woman herself at a few of Josie's get togethers.

'Well, I'm treating myself to a facial before baby-sitting Charlotte for the night,' Bubbles told us.

'Good for you, Bubs. Spoil yourself, why not!' I chirped.

The rest of the night passed pleasantly, enjoying another drink then coffee. It had been great to catch up.

# CHAPTER FOUR

## Grey Twilight

**Two days later**

As Hen awoke, she realised it was 'the Sunday,' the once-a-month Sunday that she dreaded. She rolled over, groaned, pulling the pillow over her tousled head. *Let it rain, pour, thunder, any excuse not to go.*

Hen lay there beside her still sleeping husband. She knew Jim was asleep, not just dozing, as he was snoring softly, that quieter morning snore she had listened to for forty years now. His late-night snores offered up a different tone, a more invasive, certainly more annoying, sleep-shattering timbre. Often during these hours, she would sigh in desperation and toddle off with her pillow for company to another bed, the one in the guest room or the day bed in the sunroom. It depended on the season and what level of darkness and comfort she felt like. But last night she had managed to drift off and sleep here beside him all night. When Jim woke to find her there next to him, he would mutter, 'Just as it should be' and gather her in a warm man -smelling hug.

Half an hour passed, her mind not at rest but tossing over this thought and that, what she had to do before she left to drive the forty minutes to Twilight Time Nursing Home. Those old biddies, she thought, propped up in bed for a three-course breakfast before even eight o clock. She did not know how her wheelchair ridden mother of eighty-seven could do justice to the meals she tucked into. The thought of porridge, eggs and bacon, yoghurt, stewed fruit, and toast so early in the day repulsed her. A piece of fruit and a coffee was all she could tolerate first thing and that only after showering and dressing.

Hen sighed, thinking of the morning ahead. She could not avoid the inevitable any longer, so rose quietly from the bed so as not to awaken Jim and padded with bare feet to the bathroom.

Fifteen minutes later, she emerged. A glance in the mirror, as she passed into the hall, met with her approval. Tidy short hair coordinated navy spotted shirt, navy blue slacks. Yes, she would pass muster. She was presentable, suitably attired, and coiffed for inspection by Edith, her eagle-eyed mother. Even though Hen was in her sixties, visiting her mother made her feel like a child again. Edith would appraise her and especially Hen's sister, Josie, from head to foot as soon as they stepped into room 15, East wing.

Her mother always requested she bring biscuits, chocolate, sweets, and toiletries each visit. Collecting these, Hen set off out the side door into the garage. She opened the car with the resounding click of the remote control. Once settled inside, mirror adjusted, seatbelt on, she reversed out and was on the way out of her 'over fifties' villa complex and off to 'see Mother.' As she drove the familiar route, her car seemed to go into auto pilot, leaving her mind blank and free to wonder.

How many more months, years, decades did she have to make this pilgrimage to the old lady? Would her mother ever fall off her perch? It seemed not. This caring and fawning to her irascible, ungrateful parent seemed endless, stretching from when Hen was a young woman herself, with toddlers and babies demanding her thirty-year-old attention. Her mother had always been demanding of her daughters and of her own long-suffering husband, Arthur, Hen's father.

Diagnosed with Multiple Sclerosis almost fifty years ago, Edith had conveniently cast herself as a victim, an invalid, and settled into half a century of barking commands, mostly of the fetching kind, 'Bring me my brush, my pills, my jumper, oh and a glass of water for the pills dear, and a cup of tea would be nice too.' There never was a 'please' or 'thank you' to accompany these demands or their execution. Edith expected and obviously enjoyed being the central cog in her home around which others scurried to her bidding. Poor Dad, Hen thought, not for the first time. How had he stood it?

Well, he hadn't in the end, she conceded. He possibly had developed dementia as a much-needed refuge from the mental harassment delivered by his wife. But dear old Dad, was finally at peace, she hoped, even though he was still technically in room 15 with Mother. Well not all of him, just his remnants, the hardier parts that survived the crematorium furnace. Her father now resided, resting, she hoped, in a green urn on a shelf opposite her mother's bed. Arthur's ashes awaited Edith's passing. When the old woman's time ran out, if it ever did, their ashes would be combined forever and suitably scattered. She and Josie had often chuckled as to whether Dad was spiritually shrieking in his now silent, ashen voice,

'No, no, get me out of here, away from her!'

Should they have just scattered him beside a river as he had requested, alone to waft away into the welcoming ether, away and at peace at last? They could even now, sneak his old bones out of room 15 and dispense him to the soft breeze.

Edith had decided otherwise though. She kept an eagle eye on Arthur in the green urn just as she had when he was with her in the flesh.

'He will stay with me here, as it should be. We have been together seventy years. We can't be apart now. He will wait for me and be happy when I join him. We will be as one again, as it should be.'

Edith had a very fixed view of the world and how 'it should be.'

Somehow, despite Hen's daydreaming, the car delivered her to her destination. The usual parking spot near the front door of the home was vacant. Families visited their 'loved ones' regularly after their admission but then the visits dropped off becoming less and less frequent. Staff had informed Hen that some residents, as they called the oldies interred here, received no visitors. Sundays, despite surely being an ideal day for working people to visit, never seemed that popular. Let's face it, why would there be a queue to visit such a place?

Ah, there was her sister, Josie. She recognized the flash of colour, out the corner of her eye. Josie's little yellow VW nosed in beside Hen's car and her sister soon clambered out of the small car with a cheery wave and grin. Hen hauled herself out of her larger and higher Lexus, collected the basket of goods for her mother, her handbag, the keys and walked around the car to meet her sister.

Josie, like her car, was a flash of colour. Never one for basics, for colour co-ordination and certainly not a fan of beige or white linen, Josie brightened any day with her wardrobe of hippy mismatches. Today she wore a green singlet under an elephant emblazoned open shirt of cerise, complemented by an Indian cotton turquoise flowing skirt that had seen better days.

Seeing Hen's cursory glance of her attire, Josie laughed and explained,

'Oh, I had to dress comfortably because I brought Zoe along,' even though her dress style was always comfortable.

Zoe was Josie's Maltese-cross dog, now middle-aged and though still adorably cute, snappy at times in a typical middle-aged way. The back door of Josie's VW opened to the flurry of excited barking and tail wagging as Zoe jumped down to greet Hen. Zoe had sorted through her doggy scent memory and there near the top, in the frequent use section was the scent of Hen, a nice friendly, caring scent when described in canine terms.

Josie tried to juggle a plastic Tupperware container of Jatz crackers with cheese and tomato on top, her mother's favourite, whilst trying to steer Zoe on her lead, pink with spangled paw prints, across the car park.

Hen pressed the entry code required at the nursing home front entrance and *Beep*, they were in. Zoe, excitement at fever pitch, pulled Josie along. Though small, Zoe displayed draught horse strength at times like these. Just like Hen's car, Zoe knew the way, courtesy of another of her doggy frequently used scents.

Dragged along by a huffing Zoe, Josie chatted with her sister, smoothing her blonde frizzy, now greying shoulder length hair in anticipation of the imminent Mother inspection. Josie's hair never passed inspection, though, so why bother to smooth it, Hen wondered. It only bounced back in defiance. They entered room 15 in a flurry of doggy exuberance and with the savoury crackers in a state of disarray.

Edith sat in her usual spot by the closed French doors of room 15 that overlooked the garden courtyard. Hunched over in her wheelchair, the extra-large size for big ladies, she was bundled in an assortment of mismatched clothing. Because of this hurried dressing by a time poor nurse, Edith looked like a homeless bag lady.

With a woollen crocheted granny rug over her knees that fell to her pink bed-socked feet, Edith peered up to appraise her daughters, ridiculous really considering how she looked herself. But Edith never saw herself as others did, an ordinary overweight old lady. No, Edith saw herself as a woman of class and wealth who happened by a cruel twist of fortune to be in a place of care with 'grubby old women' as she called them.

'Now, Josie you really should get a decent haircut, wearing your hair like that at your age, what are you thinking of?' she barked.

Josie muttered to herself and rolled her eyes at her sister, who smiled back empathetically. Mother never changed.

'Once the hair police, always the hair police', Josie said to herself.

In fact, Josie had suffered over fifty years of hair policing from her mother. Apart from the bowl haircuts of her childhood inflicted upon her by her insistent mother in the kitchen, Josie's hair had never met the stamp of Mother approval.

It was not just the hair department that Josie failed dismally in but the clothes and the husband departments too.

'What is that you are wearing? Are they elephants on your shirt? Surely not, Josie, at your age?' Edith queried. She peered at Josie over her finger-print smeared glasses.

'Don't you have an iron, dear? Look, you are all creased, and that skirt, what a colour to wear with green and cherry, my heavens, Josie!'

Zoe as if saddened by criticism of her much-loved mistress, whimpered in sympathy.

To sabotage the dressing down of her sister, Hen piped up, 'Look what we have brought you, Mum!' and started to unload the provisions and treats.

Edith's eagle-eyed vision switched abruptly to the containers of food, shampoo and talcum powder laid out before her on the wheel alongside table.

'And I brought you the Jatz you like, Mum,' Josie added, placing the savouries on the table near her mother. Edith surveyed the offering, now jumbled up with tomato slices askew, thanks to Zoe.

She wriggled forward in her wheelchair and mouth already chomping, settled in for a feed. In went the savouries, one after the other, into her yellow toothed mouth. Crumbs flew freely as she continued to berate Josie on her appearance, totally oblivious of her own dishevelled one.

When the morning tea trolley arrived, Edith barked her beverage order at the pretty young catering aide. The young woman cheerfully deposited a mug of warm milo next to the sweets and chocolates on Edith's tray and passed Josie and Hen a complimentary coffee. It was a small reward for enduring a visit.

Hen and Josie always came together now, to fortify each other. The visits were less frequent too, only once a month now. They used to be weekly, then fortnightly, but after six long years of visiting, monthly was all the sisters could manage. They, after all, were getting old themselves.

At times like this, the sisters, still treated like children by their mother, found it hard to believe they were both well past middle age. How had it come to be? It seemed only yesterday that they were young mothers and before that, lovers, and girlfriends and even before that, groovy teenagers. But a glance in any mirror now, especially those terrible fluorescent lit ones in the ladies' toilets at the shops, confirmed the sad truth. They were older women now, approaching senior citizen status. Overnight it had seemed they were joining the invisible people, the old grey people that no-one noticed at the shops, on the street, anywhere really.

# CHAPTER FIVE

# Red is the colour of arguments

**Josie and Max argued that week**

'I'm not comfortable with these new schemes of yours, especially the Excita one. I won't invite any of my friends. No, I just won't Max.' Josie announced.

'Well, we won't get a lifestyle like the Millers, if you refuse to support me.'

'I don't want to be like the Millers, Gloria especially. She is a fake plastic cut-out, one of your groupies!'

'How dare you call her that, a groupie! They are my friends, my role models. We can be Gold Diamond like them and live the dream!'

'Max! Dreams and schemes, that's all you ever think about! You had the dream, your father's house, plenty of money, shops, flats. You had it all at thirty. Now we have lost it all because of your dreams. Your schemes just lose money, fail dismally. Why can't you just work like other men, provide a reliable income?'

Josie knew she had gone too far this time. She could see Max's anger rising. His eyes blinked rapidly, his face grew bright pink. He glared at her through his smeared glasses.

'That sort of work is slavery, servitude to someone else's business. I like to be my own boss, in control,' he retorted.

'But you aren't in control. All these businesses are pyramid schemes, owned by someone else, some big entity that can go bust at any moment, as they do. Those at the top don't care about the little minions who buy in. They just exploit them. You know how many have let you down after you thought you were building an empire. What about the last few and ones before that? It's why each week, each month you have a new one. I'm over all this, Max. It's too stressful!'

'How dare you call them pyramids! You are just as ignorant as the rest. Haven't you learnt anything listening to all those tapes in the car and coming to the conferences? And I do all the work. I slave away all day finding prospects, designing flyers, making calls, sending emails. You don't see how much I do.' 'And you've never seen what I do either, Max. I practically raised the kids as a single parent because where were you? In the office, in front of that screen.'

'I was working like the other husbands. I was trying to establish a passive income.'

'But the other husbands bring home a pay packet, a regular income. I feel we are going backwards, not forwards. You could have put all your dad's money in the bank, rented his house and sat back while it grew in value. Instead, you have gambled it away.'

'Rubbish, who has told you that? It's not true. We are on the way to Gold Diamond with the Millers. We will have a lifestyle like the rich and famous! This new one is so good, Josie. We can do it together, reach Gold Diamond like the Millers!' he implored.

Josie appraised her seemingly crazed husband. His eyes blinked behind his foggy, smeared glasses. *What a sad old fellow he has become. Dirty glasses, grubby T-shirt, track pants bagged at the knee. What happened to the suave, debonair charmer who stole my heart twenty years ago? Max has lost his mind, surely. He is obsessed with the Millers.*

She despised the Millers. Even the first time she met them at one of those 'Ra-Ra! Let's get rich quick' conferences, she had seen through their masks. Brax Miller took centre stage with his shiny well-cut suit and polished loafers and his forced smile. He was a phony like his plastic, glittery wife. Gloria had reeked of some overly floral perfume when she had leaned in to greet Josie that first time. Josie knew Gloria viewed Max as fresh fodder for the pyramid. All the little people sucked in by the promise of an unobtainable dream fed into Gloria and Brax's income at the top.

The worst part about all these schemes was that Max constantly wanted 'prospects' for them. How many friends had they lost because of this? How many times had he forced Josie to prospect her friends, invite them over with the promise, 'We have a wonderful business opportunity we'd like to share with you, would Monday or Tuesday evening suit?'

After they came, many of them broke off contact. Yes, she had lost many friends that way. That is why she refused to invite the ones she had left. Bubbles and I, to our credit, did not reject her because of Max. We had come along to a few opportunities but had politely declined the 'wonderful offer' and left without signing up.

'Max, this can't go on. We can't go on like this. It's your dream, not mine, this obsession with the Millers. All the dreams, the whole twenty odd years of them have been your dreams, never mine. I didn't sign up for this madness. I can't do it anymore.'

There, she had finally said it, found her voice.

Max sat still, rigid, blinking furiously, shocked by Josie's words.

'You don't understand! You want to live in ignorance, in slavery like the others who refuse to believe!' he raged.

'Max, this is slavery. Multi-level is like a cult. It has you in its claws. I want to break free. I want my life back.'

Her husband glared at her. If looks could kill, Max had the look.

Josie left him there in his 'office.' Having delivered her message, she needed air, fresh air, not the stale, musty odour of this room. He never opened the windows and today to add to the staleness was the smell of anger mingled with Max's sweat.

She passed through the house and into the garden. It was her refuge. The back porch was delightfully sunny at this time of the day. Zoe was already there in her wicker bed. She looked up at her mistress, sighed and snuggled back into her soft blanket.

'Hey, little one, there you are. Best spot isn't it. Rather than sit down, Josie felt the need to walk. She headed past the vegetable patch to the guinea pig cage. Miss Betty and Miss Brown were out of their wooden cave and nibbling the grass. They like Zoe, looked up, expectedly. Usually, Josie had some scraps to give them but because she was upset, she had forgotten to collect the vegie scraps from the kitchen. The small animals squeaked for their scraps.

'Sorry, girls, I forgot. That crazy man distracted me. Later, I'll bring them over later,' she told them.

Somehow, the little pets understood and returned to their grazing. Josie made a tour of her garden, snapping dry flower heads and out of place twiggy stalks, as if each one was Max's head.

'Silly, silly man,' she muttered.

# CHAPTER SIX

## The Men in Blue visit

The two stern faced police looked very out of place seated on the pink floral sofa by the window. They had arrived unannounced at my salon, The older of the two men in blue glanced scornfully at the women's magazines piled before him on the coffee table. Sensing their discomfort in such a feminine environment, I offered my unexpected visitors a coffee.

They declined. I was grateful as a perm client was due soon and I just wanted these men gone, the sooner the better. Police in my salon did not look or feel good. I would have preferred a home visit. But, seeing they were already here, I resigned myself to the interview and sat down opposite the men on a chrome salon stool. Anything to find Josie.

'Did your friend say anything about going away? Did you see her the day she disappeared?' the younger policeman asked. His colleague cleared his throat and tried to look important. This was difficult, seeing he was sinking into the soft confines of the pink sofa.

'No,' I answered.

'Would she, in your opinion, leave suddenly with no notice?'

I considered this question. Josie had been upset lately about Max's financial dealings. But this was not new. Things had been bad before over the years. Were they worse now? It was not my business to know this.

Sensing my reluctance, the older man repeated the question.

'I am not sure, gentlemen. Josie was often stressed about her husband's financial dealings, but I am not sure if things were worse lately. Josie did not share all the details. She was embarrassed about Max. You will have to ask Max, if he will tell you…,' I answered honestly.

The men acknowledged my answer with a nod. Was it a knowing nod? Had they already sussed out Max as a bluffer, as a self-important man in denial of reality?

I sipped my cold coffee. My coffees were always cold by the time I got to them. I waited for the next question.

'Would your friend take her dog with her if she left?'

'Absolutely. Josie loved her dog and all animals, really.'

They nodded again, cleared their throats authoritively and made a move to rise from the sofa. Their bulk made it somewhat difficult. I suppressed a smile by sipping my coffee.

'Well, Tanya, if you think of anything else, please contact us on this number.'

The younger cop (who I secretly had named Butt Head due to his large head and crew cut) handed me a business card. I thanked the men, flashed a smile their way and walked them to the door.

# CHAPTER SEVEN

# Aqua, the colour of water

Bubbles loved her job at the Aqua Tropicana. Although she only worked three days a week, she was passionate about her role as 'fish caretaker.' She had studied marine biology at university but never finished her final years because of her pregnancy. After that, her life deviated from its intended plan of snorkeling in tropical turquoise waters. She had envisaged a scientific career but instead spent her days child-rearing in suburban Brisbane. Unexpected motherhood forced her to abandon dreams of a posting in Fiji, The Maldives or Seychelles studying rare exotic fish species.

She had been angry, raging inwardly, 'Damn my body!' It had let her down. She and Martin had only become over-amorous once in the back of his panel van but her life changed forever. No wonder they called such vans 'sin bins'. One shag and your life disappeared down the toilet. Well, so it had seemed at the time. But it could have been worse. She loved Marty and believed that he loved her and once the baby came, she loved him too, then since they had already started a family, they kept going and had another baby.

'Let's get the baby years over, then who knows, I can still finish university and have my career,' she had told Marty.

He agreed and so along came Samantha, a little sister for Troy making their family complete. The years passed by, her precious twenties, in a fog of nappies, bottles and a house littered with toys. Bubbles emerged at twenty-eight, exhausted, to wonder at the speed with which her life was passing. Somewhere along the way, she had misplaced herself and lost Marty. He took off with a cute young secretary from work and she was suddenly alone without direction, a single mother now, with even less time for herself.

Bubbles bubbled along although strictly speaking, she was not a bubbler then nor even a Bubbles. The name came later after she met Brad. He was responsible for her happy effervescence and the resultant nick name, that like many pet names stuck because of its aptness. Before Brad, she was Bell or Linda and to Marty, just 'Babe,' an appellation she now loathed whenever she overheard a man referring to a woman in that way. With Brad, Belinda found herself again, found her inner sparkle and direction even though it was not towards a far-flung exotic isle. It was however a way forward.

By the time Bubbles met Brad, also a single parent, her children were in their early teens. They joined forces to form a family of seven, to finish raising their Brady Bunch of five. With four teenagers and one tween, the household ran to a chaotic schedule. Bubbles opted for a part-time job, rather than her previous full time clerical work.

The three day a week aquarium position was perfect. The Aqua Tropicana, set on the juxtaposition of two busy roads was definitely a far cry from The Maldives or Seychelles, but once inside the atmosphere of downtown concrete disappeared, replaced by bubbling tanks of swirling fish of all colours.

The solid wood entry door with a head height port hole helped the transition. Painted a bold blue with the twirled name of the store, it featured painted fish in a rainbow of colours. Bubbles stopped to appreciate the door, the day she came for the interview. It was a cheerful, inviting door, she decided, a door offering promise of 'the wonders and mysteries of the sea.'

The store owner soon realised the worth of his new employee as Bubbles with her 'almost' degree in marine biology, knew about fish and their required environment and was quick to learn the maintenance routine for the many tanks. Bubbles expertly checked the nitrates, nitrites, pH, and ammonia levels of the tank waters each day, performed the weekly quarter volume water replacements and rinsed the filters. The fish thrived under her care.

Every Tuesday, new stock arrived, and this was the biggest challenge. Due to the long transit time from Singapore, the fish often arrived in a poor state in plastic bags putrid with their own waste. She immediately placed them in clean water in a recovery tank at the back of the store away from bright light and noise. Most survived but sadly some beautiful fish, often just babies, died of shock.

'Why do the fish have to come from Singapore?' she had asked the owner, enraged at this sorry situation. 'Don't we have fish here in Australia?'

'We used to buy locally, but it is cheaper to buy from Asia and now because of this, the Australian suppliers have shut shop, unable to compete,' he answered.

'Well, how stupid is that? And so, these poor fish must travel days in bags filling with their own waste and arrive half dead and in shock.'

'Yes, unfortunately, that is how it is,' he replied with finality.

Bubbles felt upset, felt despair at the ways of man that used animals for their own greed, without a thought of their suffering. It made her more determined to save the weekly arrivals.

Working at the rear of the store, Bubbles was carefully sampling the largest well stocked pond for nitrates when the police arrived. Wearing a plastic apron over her clothes, sleeves rolled up and damp, hair in a tangled impromptu bun, Bubbles did not present as her usual glamorous self.

I had texted her earlier to warn her that she may get a visit from the police, but Bubbles had not expected it so soon. The men in blue were obviously doing the rounds of Josie's contacts. The visitors were the same police that had visited me just a few hours before. Bubbles felt flustered at their arrival in her place of work. The store owner raised an eyebrow at the intrusion but knowing about Josie he guessed the reason and stayed at the front counter of the store.

Bubbles somehow felt guilty about the police coming to see her, though she had no reason to be. She wiped her brow with a wet hand and straightened her back as she rose from pond level. The men asked the same questions they had asked me.

'Have you any idea why or where Josie would go? Had Josie mentioned any plans?'

Equally as mystified by the disappearance of Josie as I was, she told the two men of her lack of knowledge. 'No, I haven't seen Josie since last Friday night when we all went out together to the Elixabar in town,'

They noted this down.

Bubbles gave a terse and definite answer, 'Maybe, you are wasting your time asking me.'

The senior of the two glared at her but continued. 'There have been hints about her personal life. Matters of money, it seems. Can you add to this? We suspect that her disappearance could relate to this.'

'Well, Josie didn't discuss her bank details with me if that is what you are implying. But her husband was not the best with money. His investments often did not do well, and this upset Josie a bit. Surely, nothing bad can have happened to her. Max is not a violent man. There must be some simple explanation for her being missing. Nothing seriously criminal happens around here,' Bubbles replied, trying to reassure herself.

'Well, we must consider all perspectives, Ma'am. Domestic violence is common, even in nice suburbs like Buderim. But yes, it could be just a case of a runaway wife. Here are our details. If you think of anything, anything at all that could be relevant, contact us please, at any time. Thank you for your time.'

And with that and another stern glare at her damp and frazzled appearance, the men left. Bubbles gave a sigh of relief as she heard the store door close after them.

ଓବ

'Bit of a looker, that one, hey Serge!' joked the younger of the two.

'Yes, though a bit damp about the edges. Ha-ha,' his boss replied.

They continued their rounds to question Josie's sister, Hen again.

'Returning to the money matters, Ma'am, did Max owe anyone a substantial amount?' Serge asked a nervous Hen.

'I don't know, sorry. Josie rarely told me much about his dealings. I think she really didn't know what he was up to most of the time. Max has many pots on the boil. He is always into new schemes, that he promises will make a fortune. But like the boy who cried wolf, we all stopped listening and certainly believing, years ago, really. He used to brag about stuff at Christmas and other family gatherings. But we never took him seriously because his investments all turned out to be duds, costing money not making any. Josie told me that much. She's tired of it all. I think she has just switched off from it all and goes about her own life. Do you really think this stuff has anything to do with her disappearance?' Hen replied.

The men took physical notes and mentally noted the distress of this woman, the older sister. She was taking this hard, as expected. Why she seemed more worried than that dolt of a husband. Max seemed to be annoyed at his wife's absence rather than worried. It appeared to be all about him, somehow. This was very suspicious and to them suggested foul play.

# CHAPTER EIGHT

## My Tangled Green Garden

I loved my garden filled with natives and hardy succulents because I had no time to fuss over high maintenance flowers or shrubs. The garden was a mass of tangles, just like the name of my salon. The edible components of the garden had propagated themselves from discarded vegetable scraps. Tomato and pumpkin vines sprouted in wild profusion, tangling their way across the garden beds, and ultimately bearing fruit often undetected until a Sunday gardening spree. Often my three hens or 'chookies' beat me to the harvest, gobbling the tiny cherry tomatoes before I could pick them.

The garden sprawled out below the balcony as my house sat on a downward sloping block of land. Sean and I had no money to build a big house or a brick house. We had instead opted for a high-set timber cottage of just two bedrooms and one bath with a laundry and car-port underneath. The house had a short flight of steps up to the front door which opened straight into the kitchen and adjoining living area. At the back, a large wooden deck overlooked the garden and a distant landscape of trees.

It was home. I was happy here, even happier since Sean had left a year ago to live with his equally lazy twin brother.

After a long day at work, it seemed heavenly to return to the peace and quiet, sit down with a wine on the back balcony and put my feet up. Once the sun set and the mosquitoes started to bite, I would go inside to fix an easy meal. Since Sean left, the meals had become easier. Cheese or tuna on toast, or rice and chicken, sometimes in winter, just soup.

I had not thought ahead to the future. I was still processing the emotional confusion of the separation. I lived in the present. The future would sort itself. I was not interested in other men, in dating, but content on my own for now, with my garden and house.

The chooks were not the only animals in my garden. Two monitor lizards frequented the mini jungle. I called them Leroy and Lola. They represented the ultimate in animal camouflage. I could see them, but visitors often couldn't.

'See there's Leroy, my lizard!'

'Where?' was the reply.

'See down there in front of the fern. That brown thing.'

'Oh, really, I thought that was a tree branch!'

Visitors would peer in and sure enough, the 'brown thing' would move. The visitor would jump in surprise and laugh.

'Oh, my. It was so like, still, then it turned into an animal and moved.'

'Yes, that is their protective strategy. They play statues and blend into the surroundings.'

Then there were my fish, all sorts in the small ponds I had dug and lined with black plastic. Guppies and goldfish swam about with dart-like movements in the sepia brown ponds. Yes, my garden was my therapy along with my friends. I felt happy in my life. I did not expect much change in this simple life. But my expectations were wrong, and life was about to change, starting the next afternoon when I met Vidisha face to face.

The morning at the salon started with Carol, one of my least favourite clients. Tiresome Carol just talked and talked and talked. Carol did not know how to have a conversation. Her idea of conversation was a monologue all about Carol, well, almost all about Carol, as the only other topics of conversation besides Carol, were Carol's daughter, Carol's son, and Carol's grandchildren. When Carol came to have her hair cut, washed, and blow dried, I just turned off, otherwise it was pure information overload. My best description of Carol is 'concentrated.' I borrowed the term from Josie, the scientific one, who described Carol as such after meeting her once when their appointments overlapped.

'I don't know how you stand her, Tanya,' Josie had said. 'How do you stand that woman coming in and staying for an hour? I've never seen somebody pack so many words into such a short amount of time. She talks non-stop, non-stop. The only time she breaks is for gasps of air in between the prattling sentences. I had a 5-minute overlap with her once and that was enough. I wanted to bang her on the head with a fry pan!'

Whenever Josie couldn't stand anybody, she would say this. 'Banging them over the head with a frypan' was a very apt description, I reasoned. I had felt that way many times myself with Sean. Fry pans were very handy objects in kitchens where arguments frequently happened.

*Oh, my gosh! Had Josie's disappearance anything to do with a frypan? Had she attempted to hit Max, (a forgivable act) and then Max had retaliated by hitting or stabbing her with a kitchen knife and killed her?*

The thought whirled around in my head along with flashes of films featuring murders committed in kitchens with knives or frypans. One scene with Michael Douglas stayed in my mind, The kitchen in the film was very upper-class Manhattan, white shiny with checkerboard tiles. But at the end of the scene a female body lay strewn across the tiles and blood flowed in a pool around the fresh corpse.

I must have gasped for Carol stopped her chatter and asked, 'Are you all right, Tanya?'

'Oh, yes. I'm okay. It's just my friend is missing, and I am quite worried about her. It's not like her, at all.'

'Oh, dear. Have you informed the police?'

'Yes, they came to question me,' I answered. This admission made me feel weak in the knees. *How could this be happening? To Josie, bright, clever Josie of all people who was always so kind.*

'Well, they needed to question you as you are her friend. Did they ask when you last saw her, you know, just like in the movies?' Carol asked.

Carol seemed more excited than sympathetic. I told her the interview was short and that I knew nothing about why Josie was missing. Leaving me to my dark thoughts, Carol soon returned to the ongoing monologue about her family.

This time the focus was her wondrous, talented grandchildren. Her favourite was the child prodigy, Logan.

'You see, Logan, he's incredibly special. He's so talented, so good at everything he tries. And then of course little Caitlin, she is such a beautiful, precious princess.'

A captive audience, I listened absently as Carol extolled the exploits and abilities of Logan and Caitlin. I had heard the stories so many times that this time I just tuned out totally. My mind focused on visions of Josie and Max in the kitchen.

It was not like you had to make conversation with Carol, anyhow, because there were no gaps in the endless monologue for even acknowledgements such as 'oh how interesting!' or 'fancy that' or 'really?' There were no gaps in Carol's rant at all. So, as I just let Carol prattle on and on, I saw in my mind's eye Josie's blue 2 Pac kitchen that she loved so much.

It was airy and bright and overlooked the garden. I imagined a confrontational scene between Josie and Max. Josie held a large frypan and Max wielded a knife he had grabbed from the knife block next to the toaster. Yes, it was possible. Josie had been upset more than usual about Max and his business dealings. Something about a female lubricant came to mind. Yes, that was it. Max had a new product to sell, called Exciting or something like that. It was a gel to heighten the sexual experience and he had wanted Josie to ask all her friends along to a meeting, but Josie had refused.

She had been furious at him for even suggesting such a thing and being interested in such a product in the first place. Could that have escalated a fight into murder? It was a distinct possibility. I had thought of killing Sean for far less. I took the time to gaze out the window and noted with interest that Sean seated on his usual bench was talking to a woman. *That is interesting,* I thought. *Sean has company for once. Great. It will distract him from looking over at my window.*

I was tired of Sean's constant presence in the park opposite particularly when he tried to engage with me by crossing the road and peering in the window. 'It is very unnerving,' I had told him. But he didn't seem to care how his stalking affected me because he wanted it to have an effect.

As Carol continued to chatter away, this time on the topic of her talented son, I noticed a handsome Indian man appear momentarily outside the salon and then vanish from sight. I peered around the letters of 'Tangles' on the window to see where he had gone, but he had vanished from sight. Is he the husband or boyfriend of Vidisha? He looks about the right age for such a role and is certainly handsome. I mused over the appearance of this stranger and rechecked the status of Sean and his park bench companion. They were still there.

Carol was by then on to the subject of her daughter who, of course, was beautiful and talented like the rest of the family. The daughter had just attracted amazing job offers because she was amazing and knew amazing people. Really, everyone in Carol's family was good-looking, well connected, and talented. Plain, boring Carol must be the exception. This, apart from the non-stop pace of her delivery, was what made Carol's chattiness even more irritating. The woman had delusions of grandeur big time not only about herself but everyone she knew. 'Definitely,' I decided,' Carol was one of the most tiresome people I had ever met.

After she left, I congratulated myself on my fortitude for surviving another of her visits. I had a welcome break before my next client so sat on the sofa with a coffee from the Nespresso machine. A hot coffee in peace at last, I sighed. Feeling a little chilly, I gathered my cardigan from the coat hook nearby and draped it around my shoulders. Something rustled in the pocket. It was the flyer I had taken a few days before and forgotten. My mind had focused on Josie, instead. Unfolding the crushed flyer, I resumed my coffee and read.

*What is chromotherapy?* This question on the front of the flyer challenged me.

*I don't know, silly. That is why I took the flyer,* I replied to no one in particular. Living alone does that to me. I talk to the air, the walls, whatever. I'm becoming like Shirley Valentine, bit of a worry. Undeterred, I read on. The flyer swiftly and simply answered the vexing question.

'*Chromo*' refers to colour so chromotherapy is therapy using colour to heal physical, mental, and spiritual issues. Dating back to ancient times, colour therapy is one of the most holistic and simplest therapies involving immersion of the human body with light of assorted colours.

All light forms have varying wavelengths and frequencies so light is a vibrational energy. Different colours affect our body cells in different ways. Chromotherapy uses this concept to adjust our creativity, energy, and mood, clearing stress and inducing restfulness and balance.

*Oh, how interesting! Fancy that. Colour heals.* The last page of the brochure invited the reader to book an appointment and offered different packages of treatment and duration. The text finished with another challenge.

Book an appointment today for a unique healing experience!

# CHAPTER NINE

## Vidisha, the colour therapist

I had never considered therapy until Vidisha came into my life. Maybe if she had not sought out my services, that afternoon, I would not have reciprocated by booking a therapy session with her.

Vidisha must have read the '**No Appointments Necessary**' sign out on the pavement, for she just arrived in the salon, late that afternoon. I was sweeping the floor and had already tallied the cash register for the day.

'Hello. Am I too late for a haircut?' she asked.

Caught off guard by her arrival, I stopped mid sweep, gathered my thoughts, and replied,

'Certainly not. I can make time, now, if it suits you.'

'Perfect!' She smiled a beautiful wide, white smile worthy of a toothpaste ad. Vidisha was very beautiful. My eyes strayed from her face to survey her waist length hair. It was a hairdresser's habit to notice hair. This hair was gleaming, straight and jet black. Did it need a cut? It looked perfect as it was.

'Um, your hair? Do you need a trim or a more serious cut?' I asked.

'Just a few centimetres, please. I like to keep it healthy by snipping off the dry ends.'

'Okay. No worries. You can sit over here.' I indicated a nearby swivel chair facing a mirror.

Putting away the broom, I collected a turquoise plastic cape and draped it around Vidisha as she held her hair aloft in a hand-held ponytail. We both gazed into the mirror, appreciating our reflections. My own scored poorly next to the beauty of Vidisha. She was a vision of exotic beauty and I, a sallow complexioned woman perhaps showing her age. Salon mirrors because of the fluorescent lights are unforgiving. Many a client had sat here and gasped in dismay at their reflection. But Vidisha must surely be happy with hers, especially as I offered up my face for comparison.

'So about this much,' I queried, pinching a few centimetres of her long hair between my fingers.

'Yes, please. That will be perfect.'

*Easy to please, this one and easy on the eye.* I dampened her hair with a mist of water from my spray bottle and started cutting. Slivers of jet-black hair fell to my feet.

'So, you are a psychologist?' I asked, attempting some small talk. It was my custom to start up a conversation unless the client beat me to it. Vidisha had not. She seemed a calm and lovely woman. The words 'she walks in beauty' came to mind. *Where had I read that?* It was so apt for this vision of loveliness who graced my salon mirror.

I jumped a little in fright when she answered. Lost in thought, I had forgotten my question of a few moments ago.

'Yes, I am a psychologist and colour therapist.'

'Tell me, I read a little from your brochure but how does the colour therapy work?'

'Well, I conduct a standard session to explore your issues, then recommend colour to assist the normal mind processes. The colour is like a mental vitamin, but well matched to your psyche. Everyone benefits from colour in their life.'

That made sense and piqued my interest.

I heard my own voice say, 'That sounds very interesting. I would like to book a session.'

Surprised at my own words, I gave a nervous cough and took a sip from my nearby water bottle.

'Certainly, it would be my pleasure,' she replied in her beautiful sing-song voice.

There was no escaping now. I had committed myself to a session with a therapist, my first ever.

I silently contemplated this while finishing the haircut. Vidisha sat silent while my mind whirled.

I had never thought about therapy until the separation from Sean although clients who knew my situation had recommended various therapists.

'Caroline is excellent and affordable,' said one.

'Sylvia in Maroochydore is the best. You can't go wrong with Sylvia, my dear,' said another.

I had filed all this in my ever-expanding memory bank but did not act. I was too busy during the week and as I worked Saturday, Sunday was my only free day. Therapists were not available on Sundays and besides, what better therapy than a day off, at home in the garden? Over the years, clients had suggested I was a form of therapist.

'You're a gem! Tanya,' one had proclaimed.

'I look forward to coming here for our chat. The hairdo is just a bonus!' another had said.

'You know, Tanya, you are a true friend. You listen and you care!' had extolled a third.

I had cherished such comments. They made me feel valued and special.

*Snip, snip.* My thoughts fell into rhythm with the scissors. Vidisha sat silently watching my reflection at work.

At the completion of the haircut, Vidisha exclaimed, 'Thank you so much. Oh, I don't even know your name! Please tell me,'

'Tanya. My name is Tanya. I know yours because I took one of your brochures plus your name is on the wall.'

'Yes, so it is.' She laughed and I appreciated her beautiful teeth once more.

She paid me for the haircut and was about to leave when she turned back to me.

'So, you would like a session sometime. We can make a time now or you can ring me. You have my number.'

'Could you do a time like about 5pm or later so I can finish work and just come upstairs? I know if I don't make a time now, I will procrastinate, and it will never happen.'

I felt proud of my honesty, and she seemed impressed too. It was like my mind had taken control of me. Words leapt out ahead of my thoughts. That day, I seemed to run on auto pilot.

'How about this time next week at 5.30pm? That will give you time to clear up after the day.'

She said that surveying her own strewn hair around the chair where she had sat.

'Perfect,' I replied.

'Next Wednesday, then, Tanya. I will look forward to it.'

'Me, too,' I replied.

'Till then and thank you, Tanya for the cut.'

Vidisha left as she arrived, with a flash of colour and a whiff of jasmine flowers.

# CHAPTER TEN

## My Colours

I wore a white T shirt and skirt to Vidisha's session thinking a blank canvas would be best for my colour therapy. It was only when I sat down in the waiting room that I realised the T shirt had a yellowish stain in the middle of it. *Oh no! How did that happen?*

I was rubbing away at the offending splotch to no avail when Vidisha emerged from an adjacent door. *Oops! Caught in the act!* Feeling flustered, I stood up and brushed my skirt down nervously as if it too had issues. Vidisha looked as cool and beautiful as before and smiled her toothpaste smile. She wore a lovely yellow sari and her black hair hung loose down her back.

'Tanya, lovely to see you again. Do come in.'

She waved her slim, elegant arm in the direction of the open door, and I entered before her. She shut the door and gestured to a comfortable looking crimson armchair in the opposite corner. The chair was indeed comfortable and covered in soft velvet which felt very luxurious.

'I wore white today so you can recommend colours. But as you can see, I didn't check this shirt first and well it's not perfectly white,' I explained.

It felt better to come 'clean', excuse the pun, about my dirty shirt than wait anxiously for Vidisha to 'spot' the stain.

'Oh, never mind that. It happens doesn't it, when we wear white which is why I rarely wear white. Well, white is the wrong colour to wear in India anyway. Like in China, white is the colour of mourning.'

'Oh my gosh!' I exclaimed. Suddenly I really wanted to tear off my shirt not just because of the glaring stain.

'Yes, colours mean different things in different cultures. In the West you wear black as the funereal colour and white as the wedding or purity colour. Pink and blue, too, in the West are assigned to girls and boys. In Asia this is not the case. But today is not just about recommending a colour for you. I can't do that until I know more about you, Tanya. So please tell me what brings you here today!'

'Well, mostly curiosity. Therapy is not something I've thought about before. The whole colour idea interested me though and there are a few issues troubling me.'

'Okay. Well, please go on.'

'About a year ago, my husband and I separated. It was mostly over money issues. Sean is hopeless with earning and keeping money. If he gets his hands on it, he will spend it on something stupid or put a bet on the horses or football. But mostly, he is lazy and usually out of work.'

I grimaced at the description of Sean. *Had I been too hard on him?*

'That is sad to hear, Tanya, but not uncommon. It seems to me that the female is more hard- working in many cultures. She runs the house, rears the children, and often works as well. So, do you see a possibility of getting back together with Sean?'

'No, I don't. Sean will never change, despite what he promises.'

'Okay, Tanya. We can talk about healing and strengthening your path ahead.'

I nodded but then added, 'Also, I am worried about another matter. My friend is missing. She went missing a week ago. It is most unusual, unlike her.'

I explained a little about Josie and our friendship and now my concern over her disappearance. Vidisha was a good listener. She nodded and took notes as I spoke. Then she asked more about my marriage, and I found myself sharing more than I expected. It felt liberating to unburden myself. When I came to a halt and glanced up at the wall clock, forty minutes had passed. Deciding that Vidisha now knew enough about Sean and our rocky marriage, I sat silent waiting for her to speak.

'It seems interesting that you are looking to find yourself and your friend as well. I certainly hope that nothing serious has happened to your Josie. Because you mention Josie, we will do some colour therapy today. Colour can help crystallise matters. It may help you realise something about your friend that will help the police. Now come over here and sit in front of this mirror. Ha- Ha, I realise that is exactly what I did in your salon. The situation is now reversed.'

Intrigued, I moved from the armchair to the more upright chair in front of a beautiful oval gilt rimmed mirror on the opposite wall. Vidisha stood behind me just as I had stood behind her a week ago. But instead of attacking my hair which I noticed was a little ruffled like myself, she draped a brilliant piece of pink cloth around my shoulders.

'Now, there, that is better. Notice how your skin glows and your eyes shine?'

She removed and then replaced the large silk scarf. Yes, there was a difference, and it was not just the covering of my embarrassingly stained shirt. I definitely looked better in pink. My eyes seemed greener and my skin glowed. Then the pink disappeared, and Vidisha draped me with a shimmering turquoise.

'Oh, that is beautiful!' I exclaimed.

'And now you look beautiful, Tanya. This colour is lovely on you.'

I blushed. *Beautiful? How could I be beautiful when my reflection seemed so plain compared to Vidisha's exotic appearance. There seemed no comparison.*

'You are, I believe, a spring personality. Adventurous, brave, and fun-loving.'

'I am?'

'Yes. But to confirm this we will drape you in a few wrong colours. Red and navy blue, even black.'

She drew away my beautiful cape of turquoise and draped me with red, then navy and lastly black. None of these colours liked me. I looked drab and dull as if the sun had gone behind a cloud.

'Oh,' is all I could say.

'Yes, oh. Now some magic again!'

A soft, lemon yellow appeared around my shoulders and again softened my face and I glowed again.

'There we go. Now your homework is to go home to your cupboard and take out the right colours for you according to this chart. I want you to only wear these until our next session and let us see how you feel. If you don't have any of these colours, then you may need to buy a few shirts or drape yourself in a scarf. Your skirt or pants can be a different colour but nothing too different. No red, navy or black. Denim is acceptable, though. Also, think about your friend and try to not think about Sean, just yourself and your dear friend.'

At home, I poured myself a glass of white wine and padded barefoot into my bedroom. Placing the wine on my bureau, I opened the wardrobe and surveyed my collection of clothes. Oh, dear. Twenty years of mismatches, bargain box and op shop finds. All the colours of the rainbow, it seemed. But were they the right colours?

Two glasses of wine later, I had assembled a selection of outfits on the bed. I was ready for my colour therapy. I would find myself and Josie too.

# CHAPTER ELEVEN

# Turquoise, the colour for discovery

'This colour thing is really interesting, Bubbles. I'm feeling better already wearing this aqua shirt. Of course, it doesn't help with Josie. But I've been thinking. If I go around and see Max, see the house, maybe something will twig...'

'Yes, the colour does suit you. So, you will go visit Max?'

'Well, he keeps ringing me. He insists I know where she is. So, maybe he didn't kill Josie like in my dream, my nightmare really,' I explained.

'Gosh, I hope not. But the police have already visited you at the salon and me too at the shop. You and I told them everything we know, which is not a real lot. I felt like a criminal when they came. I was in the middle of testing the pond. Thank goodness I wasn't serving a customer or had a fish in the net. Even so, it felt terribly awkward. The boss was not impressed either.'

'Me, too. I had a lady due for a perm. I just wanted them gone. But of course, they must do their job. They have to find Josie and Zoe, wherever they are. I just can't believe it could be a kidnapping or foul play. The police haven't found the car or Zoe.'

'Yes, it's hard to accept. It's too close for comfort. These things happen to other people not our Josie. It's weird Josie's kids don't know where their mother is either, just like Max,' Bubbles replied.

'I'm not surprised really. Max never comes out of his man cave and the kids live away and only talk to their mum a few times a week, if that. No one saw Josie the day she disappeared. Well, not that we know of. But if I go around later today it might stop Max from ringing me all the time, and you never know, I might just notice something that helps.'

'Well, let me know. I must get back to work. We are open late tonight, you know, because it's Thursday.'

We parted ways, with a hug, leaving Demi and Dale's coffee garden to return to our places of work. Bubbles crossed the road to her car, and I stacked our cake plates and cups and carried them into the store via the side door. Lorraine, Demi's mother was stacking shelves and seeing me, she crossed over to take one of the plates.

'Thank you, Tanya. You didn't need to do that. That's so kind, saving my old legs!'

'Happy to help, Lorraine and by the way, the pineapple cake was delicious, so moist.'

'Thank you, Tanya. It's a great recipe and quite healthy with all the fruit. Any news about Josie?'

'No, sadly, but I'm going around to her house to see Max and maybe notice something the police haven't. I know that seems silly, but I just have a hunch…'

'Well, good luck. We are all so worried. Josie is such a darling and was a regular here. But that day, no, she didn't come for her coffee as usual.'

'Yes, and that is what is so odd. Where did she go?'

I felt a sense of trepidation as I drove up the winding steep driveway to Josie's home on the north face of Buderim Mountain. Homes here clung onto the steep mountainside for the sake of the expansive northern view. Once parked I admired the outlook, as I always did.

Through the trees, Mount Coolum in the distance dominated the hazy horizon and in the foreground the silver Mooloolah river wound its way to the sea. Houses and farms dotted the flat land around the river but nearer the coast, the housing density and commercial buildings clustered to form the township of Maroochydore. South of the shopping centre, the white sands of Cotton Tree outlined the blue Pacific.

I recalled the Indigenous legends that explained all these landforms in a tale of Dreaming. Maroochy was a maiden of a local tribe and Coolum, her intended husband. Ninderry, a warrior from another tribe kidnapped her. The men fought over Maroochy, and Coolum lost the battle as Ninderry knocked his head off with a club. The head rolled down to the sea and became Mudjimba island and his body turned to stone and became Mount Coolum. The spirit gods were angry and turned Ninderry to stone and he became a mountain too.

Maroochy retreated to the mountains where she cried a river, forming the Maroochy River. Her spirit lives on in the black swan which flies over the coastline to stay close to her slain lover's spirit.

My heart swelled with a wave of fondness for this great southern land and its people. With a sigh, I turned my attention away from the view and towards Josie's house. The weatherboard house sat high and well camouflaged amongst the advanced gum and lillypilly trees on the eastern side. I dodged the leafy overhang and slowly ascended the stone steps to the verandah and front entrance. From there the view was breathtaking. The whole northern coast lay spread before me, the white beaches extending as far as the eye could see along the vast Pacific to the east.

The vista at the entrance to Josie's place was less attractive. Umbrellas, sandals, dog leads and re-usable shopping bags littered the verandah, telltale signs of Josie and Zoe. The door mat gave me a worn welcome, its original cheery red message now faded and tufted.

Stepping onto the mat, I rang the doorbell, a green and brown metal duck with a bell attached below. Once, twice, three rings, minutes apart. Was anyone home? Finally, I heard a thud of feet then Max violently opened the door. Bleary-eyed and wild haired, he looked shocked to see me.

'Tanya?'

'Max. How are you?'

My enquiry was a formality. He clearly was not coping. His dishevelled appearance said it all.

'Um, Okay. I guess. Have you heard anything? Have they found her?'

His desperate tone spoke of worry and innocence not the guilt of a murderer. I felt ashamed of my recent dreams stemming from assumptions of his guilt. Maybe he wasn't such a bad guy, just weak and pathetic. A gambler. Josie had said as much.

'Max, rather than talking on the phone, I thought it best to come and talk to you. Between us, maybe we can figure out where she is. The police can miss clues. We know Josie's habits and there maybe something here that the police missed,' I explained.

Now I was face to face with Max in person, I found myself including him in my plans. He realised that I was still standing on the worn welcome mat and opened the door fully, gesturing me to enter.

'Okay, come in, Tanya.'

I followed him through the entry to the large open plan lounge/ dining that looked out onto the coast through large French doors. I noted the kitchen beyond was a mess of dishes and clutter. It was not my place to judge. I had left behind unwashed dishes at home myself.

'Take a seat. Do you want a tea or something?'

'No, it's fine Max. I'm all good.'

I sat opposite him on the couch that faced the view. A plastic dog toy lay discarded nearby. We looked at each other for a silent minute or two. Did I have to initiate conversation? As Max appeared lost, it appeared so. I vowed to be positive. We needed hope.

'Maybe Josie just went away herself. I mean she had Zoe with her. Was she going anywhere that day, Max?'

Max rubbed his hands through his unruly tufts of hair. He was going bald so there was not much left on top. His actions made his tufts stand up, making him a comic sight. I suppressed a smile and a tinge of pity for this tired looking man.

'No, well, I don't really know. I told the police. I was in my office all day. When I came out after five, she wasn't here. Maybe she had gone and come back in between. You see I have a fridge in my office with snacks and drinks and I use the loo in the laundry so rarely come out here in the day. I wish I had because then I would know if she was here that last day. That night I waited till 8pm to fix some food. I expected her home anytime but well, you know, she never did and that was over a week ago now.'

He spoke with a flat voice. His hollow eyes avoided mine.

'Oh, I see. So, she could have left that morning. Did you see her at breakfast? What time was that?'

'No, I didn't see her at all that morning.'

*How strange. What sort of marriage was this?*

'Well, when did you last see Josie?' I persisted. The matter of timing was surely important.

'Um, it actually was at about 10pm the night before. She went to bed. I stayed up late so didn't see her. I woke at 8am. She had already gone somewhere.'

'But she was there all night?' I asked.

'I don't know. I slept in my office on the couch there. I often do when working late otherwise I wake Josie.'

*Curiouser and curiouser.* So, no one saw Josie after 10pm of the night before she vanished. She was missing possibly 24 hours before Max even noticed. That fact saddened me.

'Oh, I see,' I answered wanly.

I felt sick and shaky. Had something terrible really happened to Josie? Had someone who Max owed money to, kidnapped her in the night? The hairs on my neck bristled in alarm. But then I realised Zoe was missing too. Could a kidnapper have taken the little dog too? Zoe would have been on the bed or near her mistress that night. Or had Zoe run away the next morning in search of Josie?

'Did you hear or see Zoe that night or in the morning?' I asked.

'No, not that I remember,' Max replied. He seemed surprised at my question.

Max was not an animal person like Josie, so he possibly never interacted with little Zoe. To him the missing pet was not concerning.

'Max, would you mind if I have a look around to see if anything in the bedroom or garden looks odd? You know there might just be something out of place that helps piece this mystery together.'

Max shrugged his shoulders. His body seemed to have folded inwards and sunk into the couch. 'Sure, take a look around. It's messy though. I just haven't felt like tidying. The bedroom is how Josie left it. I have been sleeping on the office couch.'

I abandoned Max to his demons and left the bright airy lounge area for the darker confines of the hall and bedrooms. The layout of the house was familiar. The closed curtains in the main bedroom made the room darker than the hall. I walked to the windows and drew one curtain aside to let light in. Josie's bedroom was not a place I had visited in the past. We usually socialised in the lounge or garden. But Josie had once given me a tour of the house when she redecorated.

The bedroom was a mess. Had Josie left it like this or had the police rummaged around? On the unmade bed, the sheets lay tangled, and a blanket half fell towards the floor off one side. From the appearance of the bedside table, I assumed the left side was Josie's. A stack of books sat beside the pink table lamp; a Kate Morton favourite Josie had often mentioned, a well-used maths textbook with a slip of white paper protruding from its pages, a self-help book about raising guinea pigs and a novel written by an unfamiliar author, Katy Adams.

I lifted and examined the books one by one. The books each clasped bookmarks inserted between unmarked pages. No message left there. Had I watched too many crime shows to suspect my friend had left me a cryptic message? Perusing the maths text, I examined the slip of paper inserted in the index near the back cover. Handwritten, filling the page was a scrawl of algebra. It seemed Josie had been working a problem. 'Try again with x as subject,' Josie had written in her recognizable scrawl next to the algebraic symbols. Josie loved maths and often sat doing problems not necessarily for a student.

*Mm, nothing to see here.*

On the other side of the bed sat a lonely half empty glass of water. Nothing to see there, either.

I surveyed the floor for clues. Apart from a few scattered used tissues and a sock, the floor beside where Josie slept was bare. Around the other side, the matching sock lay equally as forlorn as its partner. Feeling more than a little snoopy, I opened the bedside drawers. An assortment of everyday items greeted me. Josie's drawer contained lip balm, moisturizer, a hairbrush, a small torch, and a blister pack of nurofen tablets. Max's bedside drawer was less appetizing. The only contents were two crispy dead cockroaches with legs in the air. Was this all Max could offer? Did the man even sleep here?

I moved to the walk-in closet. Had Josie taken clothes? I looked for her favourite turquoise sweatshirt with a yellow hamster on the front. It was not there. Could it be in the wash, or had Josie worn or taken the shirt with her? The laundry was at the end of the hall next to Max's office. I rummaged quickly through the laundry hamper. No sweatshirt.

I peeked into Max's office. The door was partly open. Josie had told me Max was very secretive and usually kept the door shut when inside and even locked it when he went out. The office was a terrible mess. Paperwork lay strewn over the desk, cabinets, and floor. Two brown apple cores lay beneath the chair. The computer was still on. I glanced at the screen, feeling more than a little invasive. A landing page for a vitamin company lit up the screen. One of Max's schemes no doubt or a competitor.

I returned to the lounge. Max was still sitting there wild eyed. He looked up as I walked in, and I sat down opposite him as before. 'It looks like she left in a hurry, unless the police rummaged around?' I commented.

'No, they didn't spend long there. They left it as it was when I went looking for her,' he replied.

'Okay. I'll go have a quick look outside on the back terrace. Is that all right?'

'Yes, sure. Go for it. I'll stay here.'

I passed through the kitchen to the back door and let myself out. The back porch had a rustic feel to it. Its timber walls featured coat hooks with all sorts of garments and sun hats hanging from them. The turquoise sweatshirt was not among them. On the deck beneath these was a gumboot rack and an umbrella bucket.

A steel bin nearby revealed on opening some sort of grass seed mix. The guinea pigs. Of course. Josie's pets. The book in the bedroom. Were they okay? Max may have forgotten. They must be hungry. I scooped up a cupful of the feed using the container lying in the mix and walked out into the garden to the cage. I knew where it was from previous visits. We often sat outside and watched the piggies as we drank our tea. Josie loved that. Strange considering the view was amazing from the front of the house.

I knelt to the wood hutch to feed the two small animals. But the hutch seemed empty. I opened the top lid and lifted the small cosy hut where the small pets often huddled together. Guinea pigs are nervous little creatures because in the wilds of their native South America they have many predators to fear. There were no pigs there either. The cage was completely empty.

Was this important? I felt it was. Who besides a fox would take two guinea pigs from their home? I examined the cage again. The wire was intact top and bottom. Nothing had broken in. It occurred to me that Max may have taken the pets inside. This would be strange, but Max was strange at the moment. He hadn't mentioned any of his products, hadn't tried to join me up to one of his schemes. No, Max was not his usual self at all.

I raised myself from the grass, dusted the dirt off my knees and retraced my steps. Forgetting I was still holding a cup of seed, I walked straight through the house to where I had left Max. He was still there, seemingly in a daze.

'Max, have you seen the guinea pigs?'

'What?' he muttered in surprise.

'The guinea pigs, Miss Brown and Miss Betty, they are missing. The cage is empty.'

'Oh? What does that mean?'

'Well, I'm asking you. Have you moved them, fed them, seen them at all this week?'

'No, I never go out there. I forgot about them. Have they run off?'

'Well, it seems not. The small wire is to keep out snakes and there are no holes. The door and lid were down. I went out to feed them because I thought you may have forgotten.'

'Yes, I had. So, someone has stolen them?' he asked, looking bewildered.

'Well, that is possible, I guess. But this property is very secluded. I really don't think there would be any passing guinea pig snatchers about. I could be wrong, I suppose. But, Max, this may be important. It could mean that Josie planned to go away, that she took all her pets with her, Zoe and the pigs.'

Max sat up a little from his hunched position. He scratched his hair again.

'You really think so Tanya?'

'Yes, it could be. If so, she may have worn that turquoise sweatshirt she loves and perhaps the green crocs she wears a lot. Have you seen those? I had a quick look in the laundry. The shirt is not there.'

'You did?' He looked shocked.

'Sorry, Max, I did. I was playing detective. It must be all the crime shows I watch.'

I put the cup of seed down on the coffee table. Max gave it a curious glance. I don't think he had met guinea pig fodder before or maybe he was hungry.

'I know the shirt you mean. Josie always wears it. She likes the colour. But I haven't seen it this week. I didn't do any laundry. You know, I'm not myself at all. I miss her and I'm scared something's happened to her.'

Bless him. Max was more endearing than I thought. Without his spiels and vitamins, he was after all a nice guy who cared about Josie.

'Max, we must tell the police. This is new evidence. They can do DNA or something forensic to trace her? Do you want to come down to the police station with me?'

'Yes, I guess that is a good idea. Can you drive? I feel a bit out of sorts.'

'Sure, Max, let's go!'

# CHAPTER TWELVE

# Becoming Agatha Raisin and Father Brown

The police reluctantly took details from me. I was so excited at this perceived breakthrough but could not transfer this excitement to the stolid detectives. I noted their shared glances and raised eyebrows, even a sarcastic grin. But as a member of the public, I had a right to provide evidence no matter how silly it seemed.

'She could have taken the guinea pigs in the carry crate. I know she has one. It's red and about this big with a wire door.' I extended my hands to illustrate the point. 'I've seen them in it when she took them to the vet one day. But yesterday there was no crate anywhere on the verandah or in the garage.'

The detectives remained unimpressed. Max and I left shortly after.

'Do you think they will do anything?' I asked Max.

'They didn't seem too interested.'

'I told them about the sweatshirt too. It is unique because of the big yellow hamster. Surely someone somewhere has seen Josie in that and if she was travelling with the pets, they may have attracted attention too. I did ask them to offer these new clues to the media, but they see me as a nutter. What do you reckon, Max?'

'Well, you're not a nutter. Just concerned. You tried Tanya. You are a good friend. I should have noticed what you did, but I've been so depressed. It paralyses me. I just sit and look at the wall. I'm not much use now. I was relying on the police, but they don't seem very proactive, do they?'

'No. Often in mysteries it is someone unexpected like Agatha Raisin or Father Brown who solves the mystery.'

I was careful not to use the word 'crime' due to sensitivity to Max. Also, I was reluctant to admit there was a crime. I felt sure Josie was somewhere for some reason and that she was okay.

'Father Brown?' Max queried. Obviously, Max was not a fan of village mystery shows.

After another search of the garage, yard, and porches, we totally verified that the small pet carrier was missing. I believed that wherever it was, it was with Josie. After all, why would someone kidnap a middle-aged woman, her dog and two guinea pigs?

Everyone I talked to agreed. Bubbles, Hen, Demi and Dale and even my clients thought my amateur sleuthing had uncovered vital clues to Josie's disappearance.

When I next met with Vidisha, I ran the idea past my new therapist. She also had a positive contribution. 'You have done well, Tanya. I am proud of you, and so will Josie be, wherever she is. I agree it seems less likely now that she has been the victim of foul play. You have checked with the vets about the carrier, and they confirmed there was one, that it is red, and that Josie had used it recently. So now Josie and all her pets and a favourite shirt are missing. It looks less likely that someone grabbed her in the night in her pyjamas.'

'Yes. Thanks so much, Vidisha. What else can I do? The police are not doing much. They used the media the first week, but no one came forward with evidence only me, it seems. They almost laughed at my evidence. It is probably the only crime ever, involving guinea pigs!'

I laughed at the ridiculousness of it. Trust quirky Josie to immerse me in such a situation.

'You could print out some flyers, maybe go on radio or television,' Vidisha suggested.

'Actually, my brother could help you. He works in advertising for the local paper. Maybe he could post an ad, here or in a paper with a wider reach,' she added.

'Really? You have a brother? Did you emigrate together?'

'He came here first two years ago. We had a family tragedy. I just followed. It's been a bit tough on our parents back in Surat. They are very sad and feel too old now to move countries. They love their homeland. Well, I do too, of course. I love India. But I will see how it is here for a while. We may go back. We are not citizens yet, just on work visas.'

Vidisha looked emotional as she spoke. I nodded in empathy. It must be very hard moving continents and starting a new life. I was struggling restarting one while in the same suburb, same house, same salon. How boring must I seem to exotic, talented Vidisha.

Vidisha praised my colour choices and told me a little more about the fascinating world of colour.

'Colour is a language we all speak without realising. Remember the story of the Wizard of Oz? The original Judy Garland film features Dorothy and Toto blown from sepia toned Kansas into technicolour Oz. Dorothy basks in the radiance of the blue river, the pink flowers and yellow brick road that leads to the Emerald City.'

I closed my eyes and visualised the youthful Judy skipping with Toto in her crimson slippers down the winding yellow brick road. I had loved the film as a child.

Vidisha continued, 'Colour influences our decisions and enters our soul and heart. Colour is magic. We choose it when we decorate our home, when we dress each day, choose and prepare food, and buy things. Kids instinctively love colour. Babies reach for colourful toys. Later they draw with crayons and pencils and engage with the colours in play-doh, picture books and toys.'

She held up a large colour wheel to illustrate her next point. 'The colour wheel developed by Isaac Newton features the primary, secondary and tertiary relationships. Colour is a physical phenomenon. White objects are white because they reflect all the colours of spectrum. A red apple is red because red is the wavelength that is reflected. All other colours are absorbed. So red light reaches the colour receptors in our eyes. They are called rods and cones. Rods operate for low light night vision and cones for colour or day vision. Animals have fewer cones so see less colours than us.'

'Oh, how interesting.'

I thought of Zoe and pictured her and the guinea pigs seeing the world as a greyer place than we do. I felt grateful for my cone receptors. I loved colour and was appreciating it even more since I had met my Indian therapist. Vidisha continued to tell me about colour.

'Colour influences our metabolism, appetite, sleep, nervous function, and emotions. So, you keep enjoying those colours. They look good on you. The violet colour is associated with mental clarity so is good for you right now as you puzzle over Josie. Blue will help relax you too and turquoise especially is a colour of hope, good fortune, and wisdom. I love turquoise.'

'Oh, Josie loved turquoise too! The missing sweatshirt is turquoise.'

'Very good. Then turquoise is the colour for you this week. It will perhaps keep you in tune with Josie,' she said with positivity.

Vidisha was helping me. She was understanding. I felt the cloak of colour protecting and guiding me, as nutty as it sounds. The red pet carrier and turquoise shirt now seemed more important because of their colours. People notice bright colours. I was grateful Josie liked colour. Someone may have noticed her.

# CHAPTER THIRTEEN

## People notice colour, has anyone seen Josie?

Hen poured me another cup of tea and continued her appraisal of the situation.

'It makes sense, Tan. I can't see Max as a murderer unless something happened totally by accident. But no, even with that scenario, Max would come clean and be beside himself with guilt and confess. No, I think you are on to something. Running off with her pets would be a Josie thing to do, for sure. I never believed that kidnap theory. Maybe just because I couldn't go there. It's too terrible to entertain.'

'Yes, a week ago I kept imagining poor Josie tied up somewhere or buried in her back garden after Max killed her. It's the stuff of crime shows. I was afraid at first and had terrible nightmares but now I have hope and believe Max is innocent. The police are pretty useless. They have not issued another public appeal. Looks like it's up to us. We are like a couple of amateur village detectives. Not quite yet Miss Marples but maybe Agatha Raisins.' I replied.

'Me, too. I've been beside myself with worry. Hardly slept. Doing something will help us and hopefully find her. Well, here are some photos of Josie that you can use for a flyer. This large one will be good for the television appeal for information. It's the only one I have with the sweatshirt you mentioned.'

Hen passed me a larger snapshot of her sister, smiling and holding up a plant to the camera. It was a nice photo of Josie. She looked pretty and happy.

'I took that snap the day she came here, and we planted out my side garden. It was a couple of years ago.'

'It's perfect, Hen. Someone may remember seeing her if she was wearing that shirt.'

'Ha-ha She was always wearing that shirt once the weather cooled. It was her favourite. Aiden gave it her. He had the hamster put on it as she loved them. They are even cuter than guinea pigs she said, but of course are not available in Australia.'

'Why is that?' I asked.

'Something about quarantine or maybe it's because they breed like rabbits. You know, rabbits are forbidden here in Queensland.'

'But that doesn't make sense as guinea pigs do too. Josie has raised dozens of them. She used to breed and sell them to pet shops when Tasha was home. They even entered them in shows and won a few prizes. I remember once, a little female won, and Tasha was so happy but the next day a carpet snake somehow slithered into the cage and swallowed the 'prettiest pig in the show.' Oh, Josie was so upset.'

'Yes, she does love her animals. Always was crazy for pets. It is surprising Mum allowed her to have them. You know how controlling Mum is.'

I nodded in agreement. I had seen Edith in action.

'Well, I must be off, Hen. Lots to do. Thanks for the cuppa and photos!'

'It's great you came around. We need each other at the moment and let me know how else I can help, besides the appeal.'

'Yes, that would be great. The local news people said come at 5pm for the 6 o'clock bulletin. I will pick you up at 4.30 then?'

જ

Holding up Josie's photograph to the television cameras brought home the reality of the situation to me. I felt a wave of nausea rise but gulped and sat quietly with the photo while Hen made her appeal to the public.

'If anyone has seen my sister, Josie, please contact the police at any station. She was last seen on August 20, and we think she had this small dog with her. She may have been wearing her favourite turquoise jumper with a yellow hamster on the front. This photo shows her wearing it. Josie is 167cm tall, 54 years old with blonde, greying hair and blue eyes. She is of a slim build. Strange as it seems she may have taken her pet guinea pigs with her in a red animal carrier. As her car is also missing, we believe she left in her car to an unknown destination. The car is a yellow Peugeot so is quite distinctive with number plate JOS 970. Again, please ring in or visit a police station if you have any information or think you have seen Josie. We are all very worried about her as it has been over a week, nearly two since her disappearance from the Sunshine Coast.'

Then it was over, and we left the glare of the television lights for the quiet of Hen's living room.

Over coffee, I told Hen about the offer by Vidisha's brother to print flyers for us that we could distribute around local and Brisbane areas.

'We can paste them onto telegraph poles,' I explained.

'Like they do for missing pets,' she replied grimly.

'Yes,' I said solemnly, adding, 'We have to do something, not just wait for the police.'

Hen nodded and sipped her coffee in silence.

The next day during a break in clients, I ducked upstairs hoping to find Vidisha free as well. I found my new friend completing a session with a patient. She was taking the payment at her counter. I sat on a chair in the waiting area.

The client processed, Vidisha turned to me, 'Well, hi Tanya, how are you?'

'Fine, thanks, Vidisha. I hope you don't mind me just coming upstairs but I wanted to accept your brother's offer about flyers. I've talked to Josie's sister, and she wants to go ahead. We went on the television last night on the news, but we are prepared to do all we can to appeal to the public. Someone must have seen her. She has to be somewhere! How are you anyway? Sorry I am a bit stressed and forgetting my manners.'

'That's fine, Tanya. Yes, I saw you on the news with Josie's sister, Hen, is it?'

'Yes, Hen. I know it is a strange name. It's short for Helena, you see.'

'Ah! Most English names seem strange to me as Indian ones must be strange to you.'

'Strange but beautiful. They sound exotic to me,' I answered truthfully.

Indeed, everything Indian seemed exotic to me, the people with their beautiful dark eyes, skin the colour of honey, their accent, the food. They made Aussies seem so pallid and unattractive.

Vidisha flicked her dark long hair over her shoulder and flashed me one of her wonderful smiles. 'I will tell my brother you would like some printing done. He will give you a special deal if you want more than fifty. He is coming by this afternoon so I will send him down to you. Would 5.30 pm be okay. Will you be free then?'

'Yes, that would be great.'

Another client entered the waiting area and I rose to leave. 'I'll see you later, Vidisha. I have a client due now, too. Thanks so much. I look forward to meeting your brother this afternoon.'

I didn't realise then that my life was about to change even more.

# CHAPTER FOURTEEN

## *Vinni, oh those brown eyes*

I consider myself an excellent judge of brown eyes. Sean's had caught my attention back in the late eighties and held me in fascination for some years. But I had never encountered eyes like Vinni's, dark iridescent pools fringed by equally improbable lashes. His eyes met mine as he stepped into my salon. I realised Vinni was the man I had glimpsed leaving the stairwell a week ago.

That afternoon he wore a starched white shirt as white as his smile, a smile that stamped him instantly as Vidisha's brother. Toothpaste ad twins, both as beautiful as each other, though by the greying temples of Vinni's hair, he was the older of the two. He was tall and slim like his sister and as he said, 'Hello, Tanya' I noticed he spoke with the same delightful sing-song accent.

I swayed with its cadence, catching my balance by grabbing the counter near to where I stood. Later I realised that my sway had been a mini swoon. This man was gorgeous, drop dead gorgeous, matinee idol, Bollywood style gorgeous.

I could barely breathe, let alone speak. I must have gaped, made an idiot of myself. Finally flustered by my paralysis, I think I managed a muffled 'hello.'

*How ungracious of me. The man was about to extend a favour and all I could do was stand and stare.*

Finally, from somewhere, my voice came to rescue me. 'Vinni, thank you so much for coming. Please take a seat.'

I waved towards the floral 'girly' sofa, rather incongruent for an exotic gentleman like Vinni.

We sat in unison. I stifled a laugh. He was now there right next to me, this man with film star looks, so close and in technicolour. I regretted not pulling a chair over for myself opposite to the sofa so we could face each other at a greater distance, a more comfortable distance.

But it was too late. I had to turn to face him, as disturbing as it was. 'Um,' I began. Not a good start.

Fortunately, Vinni took my lead and saved me an embarrassing moment. 'I've brought some flyers to show you, Tanya,' he said.

*Great, something to look at besides you Vinni. Maybe I can compose myself.*

'These are the usual size we print. You can have black and white or colour.'

'Oh, I think we have to go with colour as Josie was possibly wearing a shirt that we hope someone will recognize.'

'No problem. We will print fifty free for you and give you a discount for the rest of the order.'

'Thank you, Vinni, that would be wonderful.'

That is sort of how the conversation went. This man had such an effect on me, so flustered me, that I spoke in stunted sentences. What a bland, uninspiring person I must have seemed as I sat tense and awkward beside him.

Finally, after flashing me another delicious smile and nod of acknowledgement, he left, leaving behind a whiff of his spice cologne.

The worries of Sean and Josie momentarily faded into insignificance as I processed the impact of Vinni. If whisky was at hand, this moment would indicate a stiff drink. Instead, I took a deep breath and sat again on the sofa by the window. When had a man last made me go weak at the knees. The answer to this soul-searching question was 'a very long time ago', some thirty years ago for sure.

I felt like a girl again, a silly love-struck girl who had glimpsed a stranger across a crowded room. Was that some song? Oh, yes, of course, 'Some Enchanted Evening, you may see a stranger across a crowded room…' Rodgers and Hammerstein, South Pacific?

But there had been no crowd, just Vinni and I, alone here in this the most familiar setting. The experience had been intense. For me. But surely for Vinni it must have seemed laughable. A silly, past middle-aged woman, scrawny and pale seated next to him on a floral couch, stuttering, blushing, fidgeting. Oh, my gosh, how embarrassing. How can I face him again? Did I have to?

Yes, possibly to get the flyers. But then after that, hopefully not. It was all so ridiculously awkward, inappropriate, these feelings of mine.

Get a grip, Tanya, I told myself.

But I didn't get a grip. A few days later when he returned with the box of flyers and the invoice, I was no better. I stuttered and blushed, fumbled the transfer of the invoice, dropped it on the floor where it fluttered to his nicely polished black shoes. He bent to retrieve it and as he rose to hand it to me, our eyes met, and I nearly dropped it again.

'I am happy to help you and Hen paste the flyers,' he said.

*What! Really! Oh, no!*

I just stared. How rude of me. Again.

'Um, really, that's not necessary. You have done enough,' my voice said without consulting me.

'Vidisha and I discussed it, and we are happy to help. It's Sunday tomorrow and we have no plans.'

*Oh, my gosh!*

'Really, that is so kind of you both. I didn't expect…'

'We can be here at nine in the morning, ready for action. I will bring some bottles of spray on glue. Perfect for the poles and whatever. I bought too many last time our team played cricket. We advertised you see, to get a team together.'

'You play cricket?' my voice asked.

'Yes, it's great. We are a great group of fellow Indians who play at the local oval most Sundays, but not tomorrow. Cricket is sort of a national sport even though the English brought it to our country.'

Yes, I sort of knew that. Indians played Australians in cricket matches. I had seen snatches of games on TV in the summer months. Long legged men in white flannels bowling balls at an expectant batsman.

'Okay, great. Thank you, Vinni.'

Against my better judgement, I'd agreed to see Vinni again.

*How would I cope? What would I wear?*

⁊ᴆ

It's not a date, I reminded myself. *It's a 'pole pasting save Josie' exercise. Get over yourself, Tanya.*

The bed was strewn with possible outfits. For a girl who normally threw on the first thing I saw, usually a pre worn tee shirt and shorts, I was acting out of character.

*Come on, old girl, just get dressed otherwise you'll be late. That would be rude.*

We were meeting outside the salon in twenty minutes time.

Finally, I pulled on a fresh green tee shirt, denim ¾ pants and grabbed a cardigan in case. I smeared on a dab of lip gloss and set off.

# CHAPTER FIFTEEN

## Pasting the poles with Vinni

'Well, he's rather impressive, isn't he?' whispered Hen as we pasted a flyer together on a pole.

'Yes, they are a stunning pair,' I replied.

'But aren't they brother and sister?'

'Yes, of course.'

'Well, Tanya, they are both lovely and a good distraction from this terrible task. I still can't believe Josie is missing. I expect her to walk in or ring anytime. You know, when someone has always been there, it's too weird when they suddenly aren't. Of course, if she had just moved away, it would be easier. It's just not knowing where she is that is the hardest. And like you said, images of crime shows keep coming into my head, especially at night. I haven't slept well for weeks,' Hen confided.

'Yes, exactly. I know how you feel though it must be worse for you. You are family. I've only known Josie for ten years. But it seems longer.'

I tried to stay physically close to Hen, lest I found myself in a pair at a pole with Vinni. It took two to paste a flyer, one to spray paste and the other to fix and smooth the flyer to the glue.

But once tardy, disorganised Max arrived, it became harder as the numbers were suddenly uneven. Vidisha offered to fetch refreshments from a takeaway shop, and I suddenly found myself at a pole with Vinni.

I became all fumble fingered. While Vinni, master of the glue spray bottle, infallibly deposited a near perfect square of glue on the pole, I inevitably struggled to separate a single flyer from the pile and if I did, often lost it to the breeze.

'Oh, well, maybe someone will pick it up and recognise your friend,' consoled Vinni, as another flyer flew off.

Embarrassed by my incompetence, I gave him a wan smile.

What was wrong with me? Normally, I could twirl streaking foils and perm rods with speedy and expert control. But now holding a piece of paper challenged my ability.

Fortunately, before long, Vidisha arrived with a bundle of paper bags and plastic containers, so my pathetic attempts at paper control were forgotten.

'I thought you might like to try a few different things. There are sandwiches and a couple of sausage rolls but I also bought some samosas. The guy running the shop is Indian. Vinni, I bought you and I a curry to share. It smells marvellous.'

'Yes, it sure does,' I replied, finding my voice. It had been in hiding a bit this morning. I knew why. I hoped no-one else did.

We wiped our gluey hands with towelettes and sat down on some nearby seats to eat. We were in a shopping area, so there was a shaded bench seat and table nearby.

Vidisha spread the offerings out before us. 'Help yourself. I collected some plastic forks and a few paper plates, so you can have a taste of curry and try a samosa.'

Max opted for a sandwich and sausage roll and Hen took a sandwich too.

'This is very generous, Vidisha. You and Vinni have been so kind. We will have you around for a meal after this....' Hen didn't finish the sentence, but we all knew what she meant. In happier times with Josie back home, we could all celebrate.

෧ඛ

The televised appeal and the flyers resulted in a few respondents leaving their names and details. No one had definitely seen a woman matching Josie's description down to the detail of the sweatshirt, but someone in Tenterfield reported that around the correct date of Josie's disappearance, they had seen a yellow car stop in the main street. The 'look alike', a slim woman with 'frazzled' hair had let a small dog matching Zoe's description out of the back seat. The witness also recalled the woman attending to a red pet carrier on the back seat.

It was a ray of hope, a possible sighting and could indicate that Josie had driven south-west into the New England area of New South Wales, about a five or six-hour drive. But was this woman Josie and if so, why would she go there?

When I told Vidisha the news of the sighting, she seemed as happy as Josie's family and friends were, yet she had never met Josie. 'That is at least something to investigate. Maybe we need to paste more poles in that area?'

'Oh, but is a fair distance, a long way from here,' I told her.

'Does Josie know anyone in that area?' she queried.

'Well, not really, not anymore. We used to live in Glen Innes as children before the family moved to Sydney. The only family around there is an elderly uncle and one cousin. But surely if Josie was visiting, she would have told us or Uncle Ernie would have seen the news and rung the police,' I explained.

'Maybe the elderly uncle and cousin don't watch the news?' she suggested.

Mm, this got me thinking. Had Josie for some reason returned to her roots, taken a trip down memory lane to her childhood home?

# CHAPTER SIXTEEN

## *Time is a Traveller in a yellow car*

'I didn't sleep a wink, last night. I've decided to ring Rob our cousin, just in case Josie has contacted him. Inverell is sort of near Tenterfield where that woman sighted Josie,' Hen told her husband.

'Hen, we don't know for sure if she really saw Josie, though. People see these appeals on TV and think they have seen someone. It's auto-suggestion,' Jim replied.

'Not necessarily. The woman seemed pretty sure, and she volunteered about the red pet carrier. That was a minor detail in the appeal. I can't sit around doing nothing. It won't hurt to ring Rob. His wife recently died so he is all alone and would probably love a chat. Maybe he doesn't even know about Josie missing. Last I heard, he still doesn't have a TV. You know, after his stint in Papua New Guinea, he likes the simple life,' she maintained.

Hen gathered the breakfast dishes, placed them in the sink and went over to the dresser to collect the cordless home phone. She knew Rob didn't own a mobile phone, only the landline. She dialled the number form her address book and heard the ring tone. It rang and rang for some minutes. No answer. Maybe he was out in the paddocks.

'He's not picking up,' she told Jim. 'Maybe he's out in the paddock. Oh no. I'll have to try again later.'

Jim nodded. He finished his coffee and took the cup to the sink. He wished they would find Josie so their lives could return to normal. Hen had been a mess since the disappearance.

If I didn't have the salon, I would have jumped at the chance to go south with Hen. But because she didn't know how long the trip would be, I couldn't reschedule my clients indefinitely, so I opted out. Bubbles, instead offered to go with Hen. She only worked part-time and could always catch a Greyhound bus back if Hen extended the trip past a few days.

They set off the next day with Hen driving while Bubbles chatted incessantly. Hen was ambivalent about having included Bubbles in her plans. She would have preferred her own silent company but realised there was safety in numbers. If there was drama, being alone was no fun.

The route took them first southwest to Kilcoy then Esk, then up the mountain range to Toowoomba on the Darling Downs. They stopped at an Esk roadside café for coffee and Toowoomba for lunch. Here they surveyed the distant eastern landscape of Brisbane from their vantage point of the lookout. Refreshed, they continued south across the Queensland border to Tenterfield. Here they planned to stop the night so they could interview the supposed witness who had seen Josie some weeks before.

'Tenterfield is the birthplace of Peter Allen, you know, the singer. There's a museum here dedicated to him and his grandfather who was the Tenterfield Saddler of the song. We can have a look tomorrow as it probably closes at 5pm. We should book in now then get dinner,' Hen suggested.

'Yes, let's book in first. It's after five. Hopefully it's open in the morning. I'd like to see it. Love his songs, especially 'I still call Australia home'. Every time they play it on the Qantas flight, I get all teary and patriotic. What a shame he died young,' Bubbles replied.

Their reservation was at the Jumbuck Motor Inn in the main part of town, an easy walk to the shops and Visitor centre.

As Hen filled out the guest details, car numberplate and breakfast menu, Bubbles asked, 'What is a jumbuck, anyway, Hen? I've heard of it in the Waltzing Matilda song but I'm not sure what it really is.'

'It's Aussie for sheep.'

'Funny word, not at all like 'sheep,' is it?'

'No, guess not,' muttered Hen. She was intent on the required paperwork, not wanting Bubbles distracting chatter and nail tapping. Hen, until this trip, had not noticed how Bubbles tapped incessantly, either on her knee, the glovebox of the car, and now the motel counter. Each time she tapped her collection of bangles jingled around to Hen's annoyance.

'All done. Thank goodness. There you are sir.'

The owner passed Hen a key and they left the office to collect their bags and find the room. It was on the ground floor, cosy and clean with a black and white décor. After a shower and change they set off for a walk to find a place to eat.

'The old cafes are gone it seems. We used to come to the Paragon for burgers and milk shakes. It was a real treat for us kids. We'd sit in one of the booths. It's now a dress shop. How tragic! The name tile is still here on the wall.'

'Oh, really, Hen. I've never been to Tenterfield before.'

'Well, Glen Innes, where we grew up, is in the same area. They call it The Granite Belt because of all the boulders. It's NSW bushranger territory, of Captain Thunderbolt fame.'

'Wow! So historic!' enthused Bubbles.

They decided on the Boutique Hotel. Its gracious old building was well lit and populated with locals.

'The food must be good and reasonable. There's a bit of a gathering but still plenty of free tables. Let's try here,' Hen suggested.

She was hungry and eager to eat. The aroma emanating from the hotel was inviting.

They shared a garlic breadstick then tucked into their respective meals, a lamb tagine for Bubbles and a steak and fries for Hen. A glass of red wine each hit the spot.

'Mm, delicious. Good choice, Hen.'

'Sure is. I'll just give the witness lady a ring. She is expecting me to call. Very nice of her to talk to me, really.'

'Yes, and I'm surprised the police allow us to do our own private detective work,' answered Bubbles.

'Yes, me too. Maybe they welcome help. The police did talk to her on the phone, but not sure if anyone came down here to interview her in person. Guess we'll find out tomorrow.'

ৡ

Sandra, the witness, was adamant that she had seen Josie and Zoe. In her forties, Sandra had a definite manner, nodding as she spoke as if to confirm her own story. 'I noticed her because the little dog in the car barked at my dog as I came out of the post office. You see, I'd tied Benji to the rail outside as I was only popping in to fetch some mail. As I bent to untie my dog, a blonde woman came around to the passenger side at the back. She put a collar and lead on the small dog and let him jump from the car. That's when I saw the red pet carrier. I thought it was for the dog, but the police said it was possibly a carrier for her guinea pigs.'

'Oh, do you remember what the woman wore, and did you see the guinea pigs in the cage?' Hen asked.

'No, sorry, I don't remember, and I wasn't close enough or at the right angle to see into the car. I only saw the grille door and outline of a cage. I have one myself so recognised the front of it.'

'Where did the woman and dog go? Did you see?'

'No, sorry. I didn't take any notice. I didn't know I needed to. She went off in the opposite direction and I walked home along the main street.'

'So, you never saw her again?'

'No, sorry, I didn't. Maybe she was just passing through?'

Hen thanked Sandra and gave her the contact details for the police again in case she had lost them. The police had not contacted her again after she had rung in with her witness statement.

'Well, you did fine, detective Hen. It seems she really saw Josie, heh?' said Bubbles. Her bangles jingled as she raked her fingers through her wild hair.

'Yes, it's a lead. Let's walk around town just in case Josie is somehow here. We can do the tourist thing and grab some lunch. There's the old saddlery shop where Peter Allen's grandfather used to work and at the Visitor Centre there's more stuff about him.'

'Sounds good. How's the song go, Hen?'

'Time is a traveller, Tenterfield saddler....' Hen sang Peter's iconic song. Bubbles hummed along adding her jingling bangles as an accompaniment to the swaying melody and lyrics.

Tenterfield celebrated its famous son. His name was everywhere it could possibly be to promote the town as a tourist stop. The women enjoyed the Saddler's Lunch of burger and fries in a café sporting Peter Allen's large as life photo on the back wall.

'He married Liza Minnelli, didn't he?' asked Bubbles.

'Yes, when he lived in America. The song refers to her, 'He married a girl with an interesting face.' She is Judy Garland's daughter.'

'Oh, yes, Judy played Dorothy in The Wizard of Oz! I loved that movie as a kid, especially the song, 'Somewhere Over the Rainbow'.'

'Yes, memories, heh. I remember seeing it with Josie and Mum. When the film went from black and white in Kansas to colour in Oz, we loved it. And Josie wanted a little dog after that. She wanted a dog like Dorothy's Toto, a dog she could carry around. We had a cattle dog then, a useful dog.'

'But now she has one, little Zoe. A handbag pooch. Oh, where can they be? They must be okay. We would feel it if something bad had happened, wouldn't we? Especially you. You are family and connected from birth. You'd know, Hen.'

'Yes, I think so. Well, I hope that is how it goes. The fact the animals are missing too gives me hope. Otherwise, why would someone murder or kidnap an innocent woman and her pets?'

'Exactly,' agreed Bubbles.

There was no sign of Josie or her car in town, but they stayed another night in case, planning to leave the next morning for Inverell where Hen's cousin lived. He still had not answered his phone, despite Hen's frequent calls.

# CHAPTER SEVENTEEN

## In Love– Sepia turns to Technicolour

It was my fourth session with Vidisha. 'Had I made any progress since the last? Did I feel better, less worried for the still missing Josie? Was I sleeping?' she asked.

I murmured some reply, trying to sound positive and thankful for her efforts. Really, I was a mess, a tragic case.

Could Vidisha sense my confusion, my dreaminess, my utter lovesickness for her brother? Could she see the change in me? Could my clients? A customer had commented the other day about my supposed lack of concentration. I'd missed applying bleach to a whole section of her hair. Then I had spilled coffee into Jean's lap. Fortunately, the plastic cape caught most of it. Then there had been the very burnt toast at breakfast, and I'd locked myself out of the salon TWICE in one week. Fortunately, again, Demi kept a set of keys at the corner store.

'Are you all right, Tanya?' she'd asked.

'Yes, fine. Just worried about Josie,' I'd replied.

But how much longer could I hide behind the excuse of Josie?

Vidisha's beautiful but knowing eyes surveyed me. She looked concerned. 'This Saturday, Tanya, you will come for dinner with Vinni and me. We will cook for you.'

Normally, I would protest, 'Oh, you are too kind. I am fine. Thank you, maybe another time, I am busy.' Some such. Anything to avoid time near Vinni. He was the cause of my malady.

But the words had not come. Instead, I nodded, smiled, and thanked her.

❦

Instead of staying home alone on Saturday evening, I arrived, flustered, and blushing at the door of their rented home. Five minutes later, greetings exchanged, I was in an aromatic, colourful microcosm of India. My turquoise dress, bright green shawl and red strappy sandals seemed at home here, though at home, before the mirror, I worried I had overdone it.

Vidisha had certainly brightened an otherwise plain brick suburban home. No white minimalist canvas here. The curtains were an emerald green, the sofa, a bright crimson scattered with cushions of gold satin. A brightly patterned rug disguised the grey floor tiles, and the walls came to life with framed photographs of India.

'Wow! Your place is great. So colourful, so Indian!' I said. Out it had come, a statement of the obvious. Of course, an Indian colour therapist would have a colourful, Indian style décor. Lately, I seemed to have no control of my mouth. I either could say nothing or say something stupid, inane, and obvious. I had become a fool. Maybe I'd always been one and it had taken a dose of serene wisdom from my new friends to show me this fact?

They nodded and smiled. They were both good at that. Gracious, understanding.

'Would you like a drink?' asked Vinni.

His dark eyes met mine. I must have blushed. I was always blushing lately. I was becoming good at it. Blushing and looking stupid. Nodding and grinning, rather than replying sensibly, with wit or humour. I just nodded and grinned. I'd become a Cheshire Cat. Vinni left my side and returned a few minutes later with a tall, frosted glass, filled to the brim with a lemon-coloured drink jiggling with ice cubes and floating mint and berries.

'Wow!' I said again. Such wit and humour, again.

The drink tasted heavenly, lemony, tart but sweet. I conveyed my appreciation by nodding, sipping, and smiling. Vinni stood by my side, smiling too. Our conversation was far from scintillating. I smiled. He smiled back.

'It is good, Tanya?' he asked.

'Yes, amazing. Delicious, thank you.'

There were a million questions I wanted to ask him. I had prepared them during my sleepless nights. Why had he left India? What was his history? Was he married? Did he have children? Did he like it here? Would he stay?

I knew so little about him. Vidisha had seen me as a client and once as my client. I felt it inappropriate to ask personal questions especially about her brother. All I knew was that they were close as siblings and lived together.

Vidisha returned from, I presumed, the kitchen. She ushered us into another room, the living area at the rear of the house. It overlooked the garden which was really just a plain lawn. Rental houses were usually plain. There were some large terracotta pots near the open sliding doors. They contained flourishes of green, possibly herbs.

Nothing much to see there. But the table was another matter. It captivated all my senses. A colourful fragrant array of mysterious looking yellow, orange, and green foods in silver dishes, set upon a crimson tablecloth, laid with gleaming cutlery and gold plates with trays of flatbreads and a huge tureen of a steaming curry in the centre.

'Wow!' I said again. It was my signature word that day.

'Sit, please, Tanya.' urged Vidisha.

I sat as instructed. Vinni sat beside me and Vidisha on the other side. She passed me a plate and cutlery. Vinni repositioned my drink so it would not get bumped over. He also lay a large, white starched napkin over my lap. They were perfect hosts.

There was so much food. Where to start? I need not have worried. They took charge.

'This is Gujarati Thali, dishes of moong dal, khichdi, curry, khadi, and beans. These are traditional in Surat, our town,' Vinni explained, indicating the foods on the smaller dishes arranged in a circular pattern on a larger silver tray. He spooned ladles of curry and fluffy white rice then topped this with smaller amounts from each of the dishes. It all smelt and looked amazing. My mouth filled with saliva in preparation.

'Try that. It is not too spicy. You can eat it with the roti, the flatbread,' he said, indicating the larger salver of bread.' It is made with millet flour and is one of the specialties of Gujarat province.'

I took a piece, nibbled on its floury texture, and nodded approval. Had I ever eaten millet before? It was slightly denser than wheat bread, nutty too. As my hosts filled their own plates, I cautiously tasted each food on my golden plate. The flavours exploded in my mouth. Spicy, salty, sweet, all at once, even a hint of lemon. But not too much of any one flavour. Nothing overpowering or unpleasant. Delicious, fragrant, wonderful. Surely the whole continent of India in each mouthful.

'Wow! Mm!' I said again.

Vinni smiled my way, again.

'You like?'

'Yes, yes. I love your food,' I managed to say.

He nodded. He smiled. Vidisha smiled. We ate.

'More?' he asked, surveying my empty plate.

'Yes, please, a little more.'

He served me again, this time adding some pickles and nuts from one of the small dishes. Now sour added to my taste extravaganza. Pickles and curry? I never expected the combinations I tasted that day. I never expected to fall in love with India as well as with Vinni. Where had they been all my long, dull life? I suddenly felt alive, vibrant, energized. I smiled and smiled until my jaw hurt.

Then Vidisha explained our dessert, halva made from boiled milk, nuts, and sugar. Creamy, rich, sweet, and served with fresh fruit, the perfect complement and end to a savoury meal.

'In summer, at home, we serve the mango. But now it is not in season, so we eat the other fruits, mandarin, orange, grapes. I am sure you will like the sweets.'

And I did. I loved them all just as I adored the curries, the dals, the fragrant stews of beans and vegetables. I was hooked on India, India served to me in downtown Buderim. I was hooked on Vinni, too, on his smiles, his gestures, and his dark soulful eyes. There was no going back now. My life had taken a different course, embarked on a new technicolour adventure.

# CHAPTER EIGHTEEN

## Somewhere over the Rainbow

Zoe enjoyed the smells here at this new place. The strongest of these most interesting smells wafted from very scary large creatures. But slowly, over the weeks since her arrival, Zoe grew accustomed to their size and begun to relax in their presence. She realised that they were not as interested in her as she was in them. Besides, the heavy thud of their bovine hooves gave her adequate warning of their approach.

Zoe mostly stayed near the house on the shady verandah, near her beloved mistress, Josie. The guinea pigs were here too in a small cage the man had provided. They seemed much happier than in the carrier. Now there was plenty of grass for them. Here, the whole world seemed made of grass.

The man who lived here moved about with the big animals either on the back of another hooved animal or aboard a high yellow monster with extra big wheels. The monster's loud voice frightened Zoe so she scurried to the verandah whenever it started its roar. Once it retreated in a cloud of dust, she felt confident to roam again away from the house.

She would follow Josie as her mistress attended to the baby hooved animal who had appeared one night. The smaller version of the larger creatures gulped down the pale liquid that Josie delivered to it in a bottle. Then her mistress would sit on the hay bale and stroke its brown shiny flanks. This made Zoe feel a bit jealous, but she tolerated this activity for the next activity was the best. Zoe knew soon they would go together to the other wood building where the birds with the most fragrant smell lived. She enjoyed this part of the daily routine the most. It was an invigorating trot across the grassy field, not too far for her short little legs and exciting because of the rewarding thrill to her nostrils upon arrival.

Each day, the clucking, feathery mass of birds greeted them at the door of the caged enclosure. Josie stepped in but sadly for Zoe, she was not allowed to follow. Josie snapped the cage door closed in her face. Her mistress had mastered this after the time Zoe chased the birds who used to be free and caught one squawking individual. It died of fright in the clutches of Zoe's excited little jaws. If birds could communicate with dogs these now confined ones would have given Zoe a piece of their mind, something perhaps along these lines.

'*We used to have a grand time until you came along, you little rat of a dog. We used to wander and peck and scratch all day from dawn to dusk. Now we are stuck in here just scratching around in our own shit. A pox on you, we hope one of those slithering spotted snakes gets you and gobbles you all up! Squawk! Squawk!*'

Josie felt guilty about this predicament. She loved all animals and seeing these once free chooks now confined due to her indirectly, because of Zoe, was upsetting. She had felt guilty that Zoe, her own little darling Zoe, had killed one of the plump russet chooks. This necessitated their imprisonment until her cousin, Rob completed the mobile chook tractor he was constructing in his spare time.

Joni Scott

Rob was amazing. She had always admired her kind, capable older cousin. As a teenager she had visited this farm in Inverell in New South Wales. Once she remembered how he had let her detonate the blasts that he set to clear some trees. That was scary and exciting, just like the day he let her ride one of the doe eyed horses.

'This is Bess, the gentlest of the lot. You will be right on her. Just sit there, hold on and she will take you for a little ride across the paddock,' he had promised.

But gentle Bess had other ideas and took off rapidly as if she was part of the local derby. Josie, terrified and inexperienced in horse-riding, clung on to Bess's neck and clasped her legs into Bess's belly. However, this action seemed to further accelerate Bess and her increased speed jolted Josie so roughly that she feared at any moment she would fall off.

The frightening dash across the paddock seemed never ending but then finally, as suddenly as it had begun, it ended. Bess stopped just shy of the wire fence, lowered her head, and feasted on the verdant green tufts of spring grass the other side of the fence. Relieved, Josie lay against Bess's extended neck, against the tousled brown hair of her animal scented mane.

The ordeal seemingly over, Josie stayed there resting against the warmth of Bess, hearing the thumping of her own human heart slowly subside to normal. The country air was silent and still. A dragon fly buzzed nearby and the warm sun penetrated Josie's thin shirt, warming her back. Bess raised her head from the grass at the sound of frantic hooves approaching. Rob rode up beside her and when he saw Josie was alive and well, his handsome, boyish face broke into a relieved grin.

'I guess you're okay, hey, Josie? No broken bones? You stayed on! Sorry it took me a few minutes to sort Bronco out and give chase,' he explained.

'Yes, sure. Bess gave me a hell of a fright. I'm not used to horses, you know. Thought she was a tame one, not a racehorse.'

'Ha, yes. She normally is just a quiet plodder.'

'Maybe it's this grass. She seems to love it. Been munching away since she stopped. I'm getting down Rob, now in case Bess takes off again.'

'No, stay there. I'll hitch her up beside Bronco and we will go back, really slow, I promise.'

Rob was true to his promise. They arrived back at the farmhouse safely.

Josie smiled at the memory of this girlish escapade and the times she had enjoyed with her cousins, Rob and his younger brother, Mark. They were like her big brothers as she had none of her own, just big sister, Hen.

Forty years had passed now. Where had it gone? Now she was in her fifties and Rob nearing seventy. They had grown up, married, had children, travelled, sampled life in all its variety.

Rob married his Meg who now sadly had passed. Cancer took her out of the blue, just a year ago. All their married life, Rob and Meg had worked their cattle farm in Inverell. They had bought the property as newly-weds. It was beautiful country by the river, acres, and acres of green during the good years, the years of plentiful rain. But during the lean years, the rich paddocks turned to brown stubble and the river dried to a muddy trickle.

It was during the last drought that Meg had died, making her passing so much harder. While she lay in bed surveying the scorched brown paddocks through the bedroom window, he rounded up most of their cattle for market at reduced prices. They just simply could not afford the dry feed, nor the transport of water required to keep them in good condition. It was mostly about water, out here. Farmers depended on the rain.

Meg's death hit Rob hard, so hard he sunk into depression. The farm and Meg were his life. He unburdened his feelings to Josie by letter. Being old-school, he had no computer or internet, so it was the only way. Mobile networks were fickle out here, like the rain. They came and went. Josie knew that the letters Rob wrote her, the ten or so pages of neatly looped writing, were good therapy. Rob wrote weekly and Josie tried to reply fortnightly. Sometimes, at a loss for news or chatter, she just sent photos, of her children, her garden, or pets.

She often wondered whether they were the only cousins writing to each other in this modern age of mass and digital communication. It pleased her though, this age-old pleasant activity of sharing thoughts on paper. Rob's letters were far more interesting than hers. He had much to report on the stock prices, the new poddy calves born, the state of the river and the politics of the local shire, a different side of politics to that followed by city dwellers.

The letters were of course sadder now. He professed his grief, his new loneliness without Meg. His children came and went as did the teenage grandchildren. But mostly, at night, he was alone. The nights were hardest, silent, dark like his heart. Would Josie come visit? Stay a while? The invitation was there in each letter.

Josie planned to, but the months slipped by in domestic routine. Max did not know Rob. To him, Rob was just a name in passing, one of Josie's many cousins. He was not interested and did not attend Meg's funeral. Nor was he keen on a trip to stay on a farm. Farms were not his thing. Max lived for the world of business and money which required proximity to a city and the internet. Once Josie told him Rob did not even have internet, he decided he definitely would not go there to the back of nowhere, to some town he had never heard of, some little Hicksville place near where Josie and Hen were born.

But then Josie decided to visit. Now was the time. She had endured enough of Max's ridiculous schemes, suffered enough of his lies and undelivered promises. It was escape time. She had not planned to 'escape to the country', though the phrase resonated with her as the name of some TV show. Didn't it feature city couples finding domestic bliss in idyllic country towns?

Yes, Josie snapped. 'Enough!' Her mind screamed the word over and over. 'Enough! Enough!' She could not sleep that night and woke in a tangle of sheets with the blanket halfway off the bed. Max had slept elsewhere as he had for the last five years. They rarely slept together. Her marriage was no partnership. It was a lonely journey filled with stress and financial insecurity. Max did not listen to her.

So, without telling anyone but Zoe, she packed a quick overnight bag and left. She had almost backed out onto the road when she thought of Miss Betty and Miss Brown her darling piggies. Max would not feed them. He didn't like their little wiggly bodies nor squealy sounds. He preferred 'real' animals of appreciable size such as big dogs, 'real dogs' not little pompoms like Zoe.

Max would not look after the guinea pig sisters. He never had. Pet care had always fallen to her or Tasha. But Tasha had left home years before. That morning, after a sleepless night, Josie stopped the car in the driveway and went through the side gate into the backyard. She collected the small pets in the animal carrier and retraced her steps silently through the garden. She stowed them on the back seat of the car. With her travel companions in place, she set off south to New South Wales and the country.

Josie loved the countryside. She felt liberated leaving the congested roads and controlling traffic lights. Being at the farm again flipped back the years like pages in a book to a chapter where Max was a character unwritten on the pages of her life.

It was the last scheme that had done it, sealed her decision. Really, it was no dafter than any of others, but it was the last straw, the bridge too far. She had reached her limit of tolerance. Health products, she tolerated, hoping each one would be the one to put an end to the parade of new schemes and the endless downturn of finances. But this silly, embarrassing Excita gel was not on.

How could he stoop so low as to want to sell such a thing? They were not in the sex-aid business! And since they rarely even had sex anymore, how could he claim to be an authority on the matter? Unless he was going elsewhere. Now that was possible. They never discussed their days or nights for that matter. Hers were uneventful but maybe his were not. She didn't care anymore, felt no jealousy if there was something to be jealous about. She just had endured enough.

How many schemes and dreams had there been? She had lost track. Twenty-four years- worth to be exact at roughly one or two a year, so they must number between twenty-four and forty-eight, Josie realised, doing the maths. After the first five years of failed promises from Max, their life had boarded a runaway roller coaster on a nightmare ride to financial ruin. Max had refused to change his ways and with each loss, threw more money at the next scheme in an attempt to recoup his losses.

'We will be like the Millers,' he promised this time. 'Just a few more months and we will be on top of the world like the Millers'.

But Josie had never wanted to be like the Millers. She did not like the Millers. Max had introduced her to them at the 'Ra-Ra, we are living the dream' rallies at the Gold Coast. Like all the winners on stage, the Millers seemed false, plastic stereotypes. Gloria Miller wore a sequined dress, ridiculous heels and far too much make-up, even for the stage. Her husband Brax was as bad, maybe worse. At the time, she'd thought, 'Brax, is that even a name? It sounds more like an abrasive product, a scourer like Jif or Vim.' Brax Miller dazzled the audience with his smart suit and shiny black shoes, so shiny, they were only eclipsed by his large shiny teeth that flashed his insincerity to the new recruits.

Though the sun was warm on the verandah, Josie shuddered at the memory of all those years, all those uncomfortable endless weekend conferences that Max insisted they attend.

'We will meet the winners, those at the Gold Level and learn how they succeeded. It is very motivating!' Max would enthuse.

But Josie never found it motivating. To her it felt like a cult, a happy clapper conference where everyone 'talked the talk' and worshiped an elusive dream sold to them by their money hungry sponsors.

No Max's dreams were never her dreams. She had sadly realised that a few years into the marriage. Max was on a different life journey that ultimately led onto the slippery road to bankruptcy. Mentally and emotionally, he had left Josie years ago, on his quest for more and more. Yet ironically his quest left them with less and less. Such is the nature of gambling. She realised too late that Max was sick, that he was a gambler.

Now she had finally left him. She should have had the courage years before. But there had been the children. She had stayed for the children, for the family. Would they understand? Fearful, unsure, she shrugged away the thought of a conversation with her adult children. Later, she would answer their calls. Later. She would call her friends too, but later...

For now, she would sit here at peace on the verandah with Zoe.

# CHAPTER NINETEEN

# Orange Flames Under a Black Sky

The fire was burning well, its orange flare brilliant against the night sky. The dark coals at the base of the fire glowed hot. Josie could feel the heat emanating from them.

'It's great, a fire. What a good idea! I feel like I'm camping, and I haven't been for years. Max doesn't like camping,' Josie exclaimed.

'Yes, a fire always does one good. There's never a shortage of wood around here. Those gums drop branches constantly,' Rob replied. He held his palms to the fire and grinned over at her. 'How about another piece of toast? I'll put another on the fork for you. It's your turn. You need to brush up on those camping skills, old girl.'

'Yes, why not? The last one was delicious with lots of butter and vegemite. Everything tastes better when you are camping...or outside one's farmhouse,' she corrected as strictly speaking they were not 'away camping'.

Though the house was only metres away, they could have been in the middle of nowhere. Without city lights, the country night sky was inky black sprinkled with a myriad of stars.

Rob loaded another piece of bread onto the fork and Josie held it to the embers. Too close to the flames, it would burn, so the art was to toast it slowly with the radiant heat of the black coals. Zoe snuggled up closer to her on the tartan picnic blanket Rob had lain down for them.

'Yes, simple food tastes good out in the bush. Somehow it gets the smoky aroma from the fire. Just tea and toast and you have a tasty meal,' he agreed.

They had gathered the twigs and kindling early before night fall, then Rob had brought out some eggs and bread, butter, salt and vegemite and some enamel plates and cups. He'd boiled a billy of water for tea and thrown in a handful of tea leaves. Then, using the 'proper' technique, he'd spun the billy around to steep the tea. He hadn't spilt a drop.

'Bravo!' Josie had said. 'Just like Dad used to do.'

They smiled across at each other in memory of her father. He had been a real character, a beloved parent for her and a wonderful uncle role model for Rob whose own father had been a womaniser and drinker.

'Dad loved his cuppa, heh, Rob?'

'Yes, that generation drank tea at every meal and in between. Tea and beer, the liquids of the nation.'

'It was fun camping as kids. We had an old canvas tent, and everyone slept on stretchers in it. The only problem was that Dad snored and we'd throw a boot at him in the night or whatever. In the morning he had quite a collection by his bed. And once a horse came along and scratched itself on the tent pole and pushed the tent down on top of us all. That's when Dad's Scottish temper flared. He didn't like re-assembling a tent in the middle of the night.'

'Yes, mostly we had beaut childhoods, didn't we, Josie? All that freedom and country air. 'Just come home before sunset.' Mum used to tell us. 'And we did mostly, sometimes with a skinned knee or a rabbit we'd shot with our sling shot.'

'Oh, no! You didn't? The poor rabbit!' Josie remonstrated, shocked.

'But folk ate rabbit back then, especially in the Depression. Meat was hard to get and expensive unless you had a cattle farm,' he answered in defense.

'Is that why you have a cattle farm now, in case there's another Depression?' she joked.

'Nah!' he scoffed. 'It just seemed a good idea when I came back from New Guinea, and after I met Meg. I had learnt some farming skills there on the plantations and well, you know, I never liked the city. A fellow has to do something, and farming is my thing.'

'It sounds very exotic, working on a plantation in the islands. What was it really like, Rob? You don't talk about it.'

'It was fifty years ago. I was a young fella, just in my twenties, off for an adventure. The South Seas sounded exotic, as you say, but really it was just a lot of hard work, every day, all day.'

'You were the boss, sort of with lots of local workers. What did you grow?'

'Oh, yes. I was the boss cocky as they say. The locals were mostly great. Happy and friendly, the odd one was lazy and difficult. We grew copra and lots of bananas, mostly for the export market.'

'Did you live in a grand plantation style house like in *Gone with the Wind*?'

'Ha-ha, no, not at all. The house was very basic and timber, made by the locals from trees from the jungle. No luxuries at all, back then. No T.V, no electricity, just kero lamps and candles and a dunny out the back.'

'Oh, gee, that does sound rough. Not my cup of tea. I prefer this,' she joked and held up her enamel mug.

'Toast's done, Rob. Want Vegemite on this one? I'll do another for me. The fire's blazing. It toasts really quickly.'

She passed him the toast and the jar of Vegemite and loaded another slice of bread onto the long toasting fork.

'You know when we went camping and sat around the fire on the church camps, we used to tell scary ghost stories,' she said.

'Like in the film, Out of Africa?' he queried.

'Oh, not quite as good as Karen von Blixen's story. '*I had a farm in Africa at the foot of the Udong Hills.* It sounds wonderful, heh?'

'Oh, so you want a corny ghost story? I have a real ghost story for you. There's a ghost that lives on the other house up there on the rise. Been haunted for years that place, ever since it was a schoolhouse for the original town. Someone died there and they still hang about. I've seen a woman in a bonnet and my son has seen a fellow in a topcoat with a moustache.'

'You're kidding me?'

'No, I'm not. Swear, it's true. The ghost is well known locally as the Macintyre ghost. This property used to house the school and this old house was the main homestead. MacIntyre dwindled away over the years. Settlement moved to Inverell and all that remains of the name is in the name of the river. My river is the Macintyre.'

'Wow! That's amazing, Rob. We are sitting on a piece of history. Maybe the ghost will come down here? Has that ever happened?'

'No, not since I've been here and that's forty years now. He or she stays up there for some reason. My son is used to it now when he stays there. I can't sleep there. Gives me the spooks. Once I was just up there fixing a door in the daytime and I felt it, like a cold chill up my spine.'

'Ooh, that's spooky. A real ghost, heh. Not sure if I am game to meet it. Do dogs sense it and bark?'

'Too right, yes, they do. The farm dogs don't like that place on the hill. They follow me everywhere but not up there.'

'I think Zoe is too much of a city dog. She'd freak out for sure. I can just imagine her running back, tail between her legs. She's scared of the cattle and they're real.'

'Well fair enough, Zoe is just a wee dog, and the cattle are huge. So, she's best to be wary. But she is feisty with the chickens all right.'

They laughed and it seemed Zoe sensed she was the butt of the joke. She looked suddenly rather sheepish and put her head on Josie's lap with a sigh.

# CHAPTER TWENTY

# The Ghostly Woman in White

'Are you sure, Josie, that you want to meet the ghosts?' Rob asked.

He worried the experience would precipitate Josie's departure. It had been great having her stay and just like old times except they were now the 'old timers', well at least he was. Josie was still in her mid-fifties, but he was now almost seventy.

'I may never get another chance to meet a real live ghost.'

'But ghosts are not real or alive,' he replied with a laugh.

'Yes, I know. I did not mean it literally, silly. I'm keen to expand my spiritual horizons, put it that way. You know as Horatio says to Hamlet, *There are more things in heaven and earth than you or I dream of*. It is good to be open minded.'

'Okay, well hope you don't get spooked, ha-ha, or have nightmares. We're nearly there now.'

Josie was breathless from the brisk walk up the hill which at closer distance proved quite steep.

'I think after this walk I'll sleep anyhow. The hill looks like a slight rise from your place but heh, it's quite a hill, really. Why did they build a schoolhouse on a hill?'

'There is access from the other side of the hill. There, you find it's not a hill but sort of level. The road is higher there.'

'Ah, I see. The hill is only a hill on one side. Sort of an illusion, like life.'

'You are waxing deep and meaningful. First a bit of Shakespeare, now some philosophy,' he teased.

Josie peeled off her wool beanie and flipped it at Rob. The pompom at the top scored a soft fluffy hit to his nose.

'Argh! Nothing like a pompom to the nose. Careful! The ghost may be watching.'

The arrival at the house on the hill sobered Josie. She stopped short of the wood verandah and surveyed the historic building. Like many built in the nineteenth century, it featured a wide wooden verandah along the length of the front that appeared to extend around the sides of the house as well. The façade was traditionally symmetrical with two vertically long windows either side of the solid wood panelled door. Five wooden steps led to this front door.

Dare she? Did something otherworldly really live here or was Rob playing one of his childhood pranks, inspired by her campfire suggestion? She had not the benefit of Google to check the existence of a Macintyre ghost.

'Come on, let's go in. We don't want to be walking back in the dark, though I did pack a torch. Too many rabbit holes and cow pats to trip us up.'

'We could roll down the hill like we did as kids,' Josie joked.

'No, I'm too old for that. I'd do my knee or back in.'

'Okay, let's go. Lead the way, Rob.'

With a wink her way, he bounded up the steps with seemingly youthful vigour. Emboldened, she followed at a more timid pace.

It was so quiet, she noticed. Not a breath of wind to rustle the trees, a bird cry or even cattle lowing. Only her footsteps and Rob's. Following him inside she realised the lights were on. Of course, this was not a haunted house, abandoned like in some movie. It was occupied. Rob's son lived here in between his stints around the state, setting up agriculture courses in schools. Rob had told her there was a shortage of Agriculture teachers and Mitchell, though not himself a trained teacher, was training the teachers in the basics of the science so they could in turn teach the students.

She pondered this strange situation, as she walked the length of the dark panelled hallway. Rob stopped at the end of the hallway, and they stood in the kitchen of the house. It was of good size with an original Aga fuel stove and a deep cream porcelain sink like she had seen in historic homesteads. No dishwasher or stainless-steel appliances here.

The grey laminated benches spoke of a fifties renovation. They were bare of clutter. Did Mitchell cook? Possibly not. He was divorced. Rob had told her the wife left with the two children. Maybe the ghost chased her away? A jealous ghost? A capricious ghost? What sort of ghost was it? Was there only one? Rob spoke of a sighting of a lady and a man.

'Nothing so far,' Rob reported.

They stepped over to the window that overlooked the vastness of country paddocks. They were indeed on the top of a hill, yet the paddocks extended flat to the horizon, intersected by a distant road. A track running from the rear of the house met the road.

'The school bus used to come along here, apparently. Remember this was the original schoolhouse. Mitchell added the rooms later. The original interior just had two classrooms. Mitchell transformed it inside to make the hall and bedrooms.'

'But the kitchen?'

'There was a kitchen of sorts here, the stove and sink, maybe for the teachers, but the benches and cupboards are more recent but in the older style, you know the laminate.'

'We had laminate like that in our house, but it was a ghastly swirly red. I always hated it because it looked like someone had smeared tomato sauce all over the benches,' Josie reflected.

'Well, come on, I'll show you the rest of the rooms and maybe introduce you to a ghost.'

Josie felt this was unlikely. It was just an old house, not even creepy really. There were no creaky staircases, cobweb infested attics or even a basement. The building seemed harmless, empty, silent. It was a ruse. But she had enjoyed the walk and now she could look up the hill from Rob's house and appreciate this place, this old school.

'Here's Mitchell's charming study. He kept the original bookshelves for his collection.'

Josie admired the solid shelving that extended to the ceiling. She surveyed Mitchell's library. Classics, crime novels, textbooks. Mitchell, if he read them, was well read, she decided. Not having met Mitchell for many years, she tried to envision him as a now mature man, a divorced father. He had lived away in Wagga Wagga for some years but now on his own, had returned to the family property.

'Mmm, nice,' she commented.

'Now, down here, are the bedrooms and....'

Rob's voice faded away as they heard a dull thump. Josie looked up at Rob. He was about to speak, his mouth half open, when there was another thump this time louder.

'What is that, Rob?' Josie whispered.

'It's the usual. We hear thumps.'

'Is it....?'

Josie dared not utter the words 'the ghost.'

She could feel the hairs on the back of her neck bristle. The hall grew cold. Oh, no, the lights went out, not candles blowing out but electricity which involved a physical switch. The thumping rose to a crescendo, like a drum roll. Josie could not tell where it came from. Behind them, beside, in front? It was impossible to tell the actual direction.

She grabbed Rob's arm. He crossed his other arm to pat her hand in an attempt to reassure her. Then the worst part happened. A whoosh of cold icy wind, a vision of gauzy white fabric whizzed through them down the hall to the front door, slamming it behind itself with a terrific bang. The thumping stopped as this happened.

'Oh, my God! Rob! It was the ghost, a lady I think, all gauzy and white. Did you feel that, so cold, like ice.'

'Yes, sure did. That's her, the lady ghost. She did the same, the day I was painting here.'

'Where did she go?' Josie asked.

'Wherever she goes. Out into the world. But she comes back.'

'How does your son live here?'

'He does. Lady Ghost never hurts anyone, only makes herself felt. She enjoys the power, it seems. Come on then. You've seen your ghost. Let's walk back and get warm.'

Josie needed no convincing. They headed towards the now closed front door. Rob re-opened it and switched the light switch back into the off position. Though the switch was on, the house lights were off, confounding the laws of physics.

Outside, all was the same, the paddocks empty and silent. But somewhere out there in the ether was a spirit who knew no rest. She roamed the hills for some reason unknown and patrolled the old schoolhouse.

It grew darker as they retraced their steps down the hill to Rob's farmhouse, the setting sun, pink and resplendent behind the western hills. Josie had seen a ghost. Her life was now richer for the experience.

# CHAPTER TWENTY-ONE

## The Brown-Green Landscape of Australia

Rob finished the new chook run. It was functional and now the new home of the farm poultry.

'It's amazing, Rob. You are so clever just knocking this up so quickly. Now the chooks can access fresh grass anytime and be safe,' Josie told him.

'Plenty of grass around here. One hundred thousand acres of it.'

'Yes, and plenty of snakes and predators including my Zoe.'

'I will clean out the old chook shed for you. Rake out all the dirty straw. You can use it either for storage or to separate hens and roosters or sparring roosters,' she offered.

She knew from her girlhood in the country that roosters fought over the hens and could make life miserable for them. Rob said he just ate the roosters for dinner. She wasn't sure if that was a joke on her behalf, now he knew what a softie she was concerning animals.

There was always something to do here on the farm, most of it related to animals. Feeding the calves, rounding up cattle, dipping cattle for parasites and the lesser tasks of attending to the poultry and now to the new residents, Zoe, and the guinea pigs.

Rob had laughed when he learnt that she had brought them with her. He did not ask how long she intended to stay. He did not mind how long as he had been ever so lonely since Meg's passing. And Josie was family and she loved to help. Besides, she had been cooking some great meals and had even baked a few cakes and cookies.

As the weeks passed in the pleasant routine of the farm, Rob gave it no further thought. It felt like Josie had always been here involved in the cycle of life on his farm. Part of this was his familiarity with Josie from childhood and part was due to Josie's easy manner and enjoyment of farm life. Most city slickers would not enjoy the daily routine.

He remembered both friends and family coming up from Sydney over the years. They usually only stayed a day or two and were then off to do the tourist things in town or beyond. Inverell had an interesting history. It had always been a mining and agricultural centre for the Northern Tablelands. Miners had accessed tin, silver and also the gems, diamonds and sapphire here since the 1840's. Grazing and crops were also the foundation of country life. Museums glorified this past and coffee shops abounded, now folk came from the city more easily than years ago.

Josie also blocked her thoughts from dwelling on how long she would stay and the fact that nobody knew where she was. Just as she had intended, she had managed to disappear from her life to occupy another life elsewhere, somewhere less stressful. What better place than here with family, with Rob who needed company and looking after? It was a mutually agreeable situation even though neither of them had discussed it.

The trip to 'town' involved a 45-minute drive along dirt roads that followed the bends of the Macintyre River. Sitting beside Rob, Josie steadied herself against the truck's door as the farm vehicle bumped along the rough terrain. Most of the route was not tarred with black bitumen like city roads but consisted of brown earth and gravel frequently peppered with deep potholes.

'The floods have made the roads worse. They are real bone shakers at the moment,' Rob told her.

He smiled across at her from his seat at the steering wheel. Josie laughed, noting with a smile that despite his age, her cousin still sported his engaging boyish grin. His brown eyes had not lost their mischievous twinkle. The main difference that time had wrought upon his once youthful teenage face were the deep lines from many decades of sun exposure. Of course, this was inevitable since Rob had always worked outdoors and until the 1970's nobody worried about skin damage by the UV rays of the sun.

'It's bit of a boring trip. Not much to see but mulga scrub and grey gums. The animals come out early and late in the day. That's when you really have to watch the roads. They dart out and before you know it you've hit them. Dropped a few roos that way myself over the years. Hate it, because I love animals.'

'Me, too,' replied Josie.

They were kindred spirits that way. Animals had always featured on the top of her list of favourite things, and she knew Rob and Meg too respected all creatures. Josie was not surprised when Rob had turned his back on his father's beef cattle farm to set up his own instead. Now Rob's brother ran the family homestead with a station manager.

'I could be a few hours in town sorting things out with the Co-op that buys my produce and then I have to fetch some stuff at the Stock and Station Barn. You can tour the shops or visit the library and I will call you on my mobile when I'm all done. The mobile doesn't work on the farm, but it works here in town. There is Telstra reception, if you need to call your family,' Rob explained.

Josie nodded. The khaki-coloured countryside had not changed for over half an hour. Gums and scrub stretched to the distant brown haze of the horizon. The sky was cornflower blue and almost cloudless. Summer was on the way.

Josie reflected that in Europe, in the same sliver of time, one could have traversed provinces, possibly a country or two. She remembered how small Luxembourg, Liechtenstein and Monaco seemed when she had travelled years ago as a carefree backpacker. Always, on return, the brown-green shades of Australiana were an assault to the senses after the verdant landscapes of northern hemisphere. So too, the high wide sky, infallibly blue, defied the low, grey skies of Europe once past its glorious summer.

'Penny for them, Josie,' Rob said, breaking the silence.

'Ha-ha. Will it have my birth year on it?'

'If you're lucky,' he winked.

The cousins smiled at the memory of Josie's dad who had in his retirement years fashioned wood bowls on his lathe and put pennies in the base. He had saved tins full of brown pennies once decimal currency came in during the 1960's and delighted in finding a penny for visitors that was coined in their birth year.

'Are we getting close, Rob? The countryside is changing.'

She could tell by the change in the landscape that they were getting closer to civilization. Tin letterboxes lined the road in clusters of five or so to mark side roads that led to properties in the hills. The small farms dotted the rising hills away from the road. There were noticeably more vehicles on the road too.

'Yes, not far now.'

Before long, a road sign welcomed them to Inverell and boasted of a population of 11,660 residents.

It had been a week since Josie had driven through the town on the way to Rob's farm. A week with no contact with family and friends, a week of freedom and peace.

# CHAPTER TWENTY-TWO

## Dusty Brown Photo Albums

Their young faces, now faded with time, gazed out of the worn pages of the photo album.

'Ha, remember this time, Rob, when you and Mark made this bush cubby. I think for you it was just an escape from the grownups, but us little kids loved it. We could never have built one ourselves,' Josie exclaimed.

'Yes, I remember. We used to steal some of Dad's smokes and sneak a puff there. God knows, we could have caused a bush fire. But you little kids just wanted to play tea parties with your dolls.' He laughed at the memory of his early teen years.

There were photos of all the cousins who had come to visit over the years, for Christmas or Easter breaks or the long summer holidays. They had twelve shared cousins in total due to the large size of Rob's mother's family, six children. Rob's mother was the older sister of Josie's dad. There had been six siblings, now all passed, leaving the next generation to make their passage through life.

'Here we are at Byron Bay. The curve of the beach is still the same and the lighthouse still dominates the point, but it sure has changed.'

Rob nodded in agreement. 'I remember the terrible smell of the whale meat as they butchered the giant carcasses near the shore. Imagine that happening now. The uproar from the greenies! Now it's a tourist resort where people from all over the world come to watch the whale migration. People pay over a thousand dollars a night to stay there. They probably don't realise it was once a whaling station.'

'Yes, it even costs to park in the main street now and you can't get a seat in a coffee shop.'

Rob stayed silent on that one. He was not into coffee shops. He was a tea man, preferably camp-fire billy style.

Byron Bay held no fascination for him. It was now a haven for international backpackers and movie stars. Some even lived in multimillion dollar homes near the now famous lighthouse, famous as the most easterly point of Australia. Due east across the vast Pacific, lay New Zealand.

He turned the page. 'This one is taken at Lake Conjola which used to be a fantastic quiet seaside town, now also succumbed to tourism and glam campers.'

The dusty brown albums showcased their childhood, youth, and later marriages. They poured over the old mostly black and white photos, while they sipped tea and nibbled the flapjacks Josie had baked the day before.

There had been fun times, happy times. Rob's childhood had not been as happy as hers, Josie mused, but his mother had been a wonderful parent and had tried to compensate for the anger and drunkenness of her husband. But once she died, a premature death in her fifties, the family life deteriorated.

Rob's father ever a womaniser, moved a procession of women into and out of the family home. The boys, Rob and brother, Mark moved out and never returned. On the passing of Rob's father, the estate passed to the latest woman and the boys, though they fought legally, lost their inheritance. It was a bitter pill to swallow. Josie steered clear of the subject. She noted the absence of photos of Rob's father, the telltale brown squares on the pages where photographs had been.

Apart from those of family, there were many photos of dogs and horses that had lived their animal lives on Rob's family farm; cattle dogs, border collies and even a faithful, fat Labrador who had been a pet not a working dog.

'The court did grant me the livestock, you know, even though we lost the farm,' Rob announced sadly, referring to his father's estate.

Josie just nodded. What could she say that would not open old wounds?

'It wouldn't happen today. The law has changed and back then, I had no money to fight against it,' Rob reflected.

Josie nodded again. She brushed a tear away. Rob understood her silence.

He snapped the album closed as they viewed the last page. A small cloud of dust rose from the old book. They laughed and coughed.

'More tea?'

'Oh, no Thanks, Rob. I've drunk so much. Three cups, I think. I might take Zoe for a little walk and feed the piggies some grass.'

'Okay. I'll come too. There are some vegetable scraps from last night and toast crusts from this morning. We can give them to your little mates. They are like compost bins, they eat anything.' He rose to fetch a small plastic bin from the counter.

'Yes, eat anything, poo anytime. I need to clean their cage again,' Josie told him.

They clipped the lead on an excited Zoe and dropped the guinea pig scraps into the cage near the back door. The small animals scurried to feast on their breakfast. They were always hungry. They eagerly munched on any vegetable or cereal, transforming it into fat on their chubby little bodies.

With Zoe at their side, they set off from the back door across the paddock. The two farm dogs trotted along beside Rob. They were not interested in Zoe. Their duty was to round up cattle, not attack small dogs.

The grass was still wet with dew though it was past ten in the morning. The morning sun had not evaporated it on the shady paddock near the house, but beyond the home paddock, the grass was dry and stubbled. It crunched under their boots as they walked towards the river. Zoe trotted along, sniffing at cow pats. The other dogs romped ahead to the riverbanks. The river was the pale brown of many inland rivers, the water carrying suspended earth from its journey downstream.

'We had so many happy times here by the river, with the children then grandchildren and the dogs. In summer it's the place to be. We floated on li-los down the river with the current, paddled in canoes, fished, even caught cray bobs here,' Rob told her.

'Do the grandchildren visit often, Rob?'

'Yes, every holiday they come. Of course, they are teenagers now and like to do different things. Michael drives the old truck around and Katie has a motor bike and a horse here. Michael plays the guitar too. He's very good. We sit around the fire like we did the other night, and he strums and sings. Katie loves to sing too. She's in the choir at school.'

'Oh, it sounds like you have a good time with them. Farms are great places for kids and especially teenagers. Gets them off the computer and phones, especially out here where you have no reception of anything!'

'Yes, but it won't be the same anymore, now Meg's gone. The kids miss her terribly too. They miss the motherliness of Meg. Their own mother's not that way. She is a hard one that Kylie. That's why Mitch sought a divorce. She was not a good mother. But the irony of it is that she has custody. We should have it, not her. She's off and on with other blokes. It's not good for the kids at all.'

'Oh, dear, that's no good. The law is an ass, as they say. Sometimes it doesn't make the right decisions for children.'

'So, no grandchildren for you, yet, Josie?'

'My heavens, no. My two aren't settled with anyone. Aiden never stops moving jobs and countries and Tasha has bad luck with fellows.'

'It will happen. They are young still, only in their twenties. They marry later these days because they all seem to go to university, extending their adolescence.'

'Yes, some twenty somethings still live at home. Some thirty somethings too. It was unheard of in our day. Out the door before twenty, for us. Hen married at just eighteen!'

Rob stopped and threw sticks into the river for the dogs. They wasted no time jumping into swim and fetch. Sometimes they wrestled for the same stick. After ten minutes of this they stopped fetching and left the sticks to float on the current down the river. The dogs then despite the many acres came and shook themselves next to Rob and Josie.

'Aah, thanks a lot! Crazy dogs!' Josie squealed.

# CHAPTER TWENTY-THREE

## Caught in the Headlights

Josie emerged from the bedroom rubbing a towel over her newly shampooed hair. She froze when she saw the television screen and Rob's face. This was the first time he had turned it on. Reception was poor and intermittent. It was hard to watch a show. But tonight, he had the ABC news on.

'Josie, why didn't you tell me? I thought they all knew you were here! I never thought to ask and of course it's been great. I've enjoyed the company so much, spending time with you, catching up on old times.'

'I'm sorry, Rob. I meant to tell them, ring them, but it's lovely here just being away from it all, away from Max!'

'So, things aren't good with Max?'

'No, not for years.'

'Well, come over and sit down. Tell me all about this. We will have to go to town and let someone know you are all right and safe.'

Rob patted the couch beside him, and Josie walked across the room and sat next to him. The towel slid from her damp hair to the floor. The tears that had never come before to offer release, now flowed. As the tears streamed, Josie, with gulping sobs, told her story.

Most of it was unintelligible because of Josie's distress but Rob latched onto a few key words that painted Max as an irresponsible gambler in denial of his deeds. Worst of all, Max had used Josie and some of her funds to promote his ventures No, her cousin's marriage was not the wonderful experience he and Meg had enjoyed together.

He sat beside a wet-haired Josie and listened, his mind reeling. How could he help? Her family and the police must know that she is safe and sound. First thing tomorrow they would set off for town.

ℐℬ

After Josie's startling revelation and even more upsetting recount of her marriage, Rob had been unable to sleep. He thought of his own happy marriage, his love for Meg, their shared dreams, and plans. He realised that his views on marriage and partnership were naïve, that everyone was not as lucky as he to find a soul mate and live in harmony for nearly half a century.

Poor Josie. How troubled she must be and how troubled she must have been during all the weeks here at the farm. He had not realised an iota of it. She had seemed happy. He felt bad and guilty because he had not supported her in any way. Why he had happily gone about his normal business while Josie must have been in torment. Yet she had said nothing. Why was that? Did she not feel at ease with him, her own cousin, her own flesh, and blood? Had she worried about upsetting him?

Josie did not sleep well either. She knew now that her idyllic time on the farm was soon to be over. The game was up. Rob now knew her as the runaway, irresponsible, inconsiderate fool she was. What will her family say? And …, what will Tanya and Bubbles, Demi and Dale and kind

Lorraine make of her deception and lies? Oh, the shame! She could feel it creep through her bones, paralyse her.

How could she return and face them all? And the police, would they charge her for public mischief, for creating work needlessly searching for her when she had been safe and sound here all along with family. She felt such a bad person, a criminal even, a lying fugitive, a troublemaker.

The next morning, the cousins eyed each other across the breakfast table. They each sipped at their tea and nibbled at their now cold toast. Rob finally tried to remedy the situation.

'Well, we'd best be off, hey, Josie? Let everyone know you are okay.'

Josie nodded. She had her bags packed in case Rob wanted her gone today. Zoe must come, even the guinea pigs maybe must come, if she was leaving now. Should she drive her car as well or maybe she should just go alone in her car, go as she had come and leave Rob to get on with his life, pick up the routine she had disrupted?

'I can just go in my car with the animals, just go like I came. You don't need to come Rob. You've done enough, honestly. It's been wonderful staying here away from the world. Really, I can't emphasise that enough. You are the best, dear boy. I'll never forget this time, here, just us. Now, I even have a ghost story to tell. Well, that's if I have any friends left to tell it to.'

Rob looked over at his sad Josie. He felt sad too. The joy had all gone now. The bubble had burst. He didn't judge her for her deception. He understood now that she had fled a situation and come to him. It would not have been much different if he had known. He would still have taken Josie in. But of course, he could have perhaps helped her more and certainly he could have notified people to let them know she was safe and well here. Why hadn't she confided in him? And why does she insist on wearing that ridiculous hamster shirt? Surely at her age, she has something more appropriate. But that was Josie, a little girl inside a woman.

As if sensing Rob's confusion, Josie reached over for his hand, his large suntanned hand, rough from over fifty years of farming. 'Don't blame yourself at all, Rob. I didn't want any sympathy, special treatment. That's why I didn't tell you anything. I just wanted to be here with you, away from it all. It's given me time to think and process.' Her voice trailed off.

'But you should have told people where you were. Save them the worry. There's been a police hunt for you! That costs money takes time away from real crime. That's all I'm mad about. The rest, well, it's been lovely having you here, especially with Meg gone…' Now his voice trailed off. They had reached an impasse. There was little more to say only action mattered now.

'No, Josie, I'll drive you into town. We can sort out your car later. You're upset. You can't go alone, and the river may be up a bit. It rained a lot last night.'

'Yes, I heard the rain. It was heavy.' Then acknowledging his offer, she added, 'Thanks, Rob, I appreciate you driving me. I do feel shaky.'

Neither of them admitted to no sleep. Rob nearly admitted to feeling shaky too but thought better of it and stayed silent. Rising from the table, he stacked their plates and mugs and placed them in the sink, for later. He gathered raincoats from the coat rack at the back door and trudged out into the yard. Josie followed, lugging her bags. Rob must be upset, she thought. Normally he would carry my bags. Zoe trotted along behind her, tail down.

The truck as if upset too, took a few turns to start. Rob muttered under his breath as men do when engines act ornery. Josie remembered how her father's temper had flared whenever the mower or car wouldn't start. That's when he swore, the only time he swore. 'Darn, fool of a thing!' he would roar. Josie willed the truck to start. They didn't need more trouble on a day like this after a sleepless night. Rob looked like he hadn't slept well. His eyes had the look, weary and hooded.

# CHAPTER TWENTY-FOUR

## *Fade-Out*

The trip passed in silence. The truck bumped along the rutted dirt road. Fortunately, the river was not up enough to cause flooding, though the creeks were swirling with fast moving brown water. It was a relief, as always, to reach the smooth surface of the bitumen. Civilisation loomed as they reached the outskirts of town, then soon they were there outside the police station.

Josie's heart sank. Last time in town, she had nearly gone into the austere brick building and confessed like a criminal to her crime. But she had been a coward and she felt one again, now. Would Rob lead the way, charge in with her in tow and announce the deception? She wished.

Instead of instant action, they both sat there in the truck on the worn leather seats with Zoe between them. It was Zoe that broke the strained silence. She whimpered. Dogs anticipate new smells and a walk when they arrive somewhere after a car trip. Today, Zoe was no exception even though she sensed the mood between her mistress and the farm man she had grown to love.

Josie stayed motionless looking through the smeared windscreen at the police station. It was an unwelcoming building, the plain red brick façade and shuttered windows were as cheerless as the day. Rain now spattered the windscreen and within minutes the building was lost from view. Zoe whimpered again.

Rob snapped to attention. He unfastened his seatbelt. Zoe barked. Josie looked around for Zoe's lead. Had she forgotten it? Yes, it seemed so. The pink spangly lead, so out of place on the farm was not on the floor or her lap.

'Um, I don't think I have Zoe's lead,' she said, breaking the long silence. Her voice sounded raspy like someone else's voice.

'I've got rope in the back. But not sure we can take a dog in the station.'

Despite this statement, Rob got out of the truck, rummaged around in the back, and returned with a looped piece of rope. He deftly tied one end to Zoe's collar and lifted the small dog out of his side door. Josie still sat, frozen in her seat. She had not even unfastened her seat belt.

'Josie? Are you coming?'

There now seemed no way out of the confrontation, no avoiding the confession that lay ahead. Josie slowly unbuckled herself, opened the old truck's door and hopped down onto the road. She followed Rob who had Zoe on the rope. He led the way up the stone steps and into the police station.

'We are here about a missing person,' he announced at the front counter to no one in particular. A woman in blue uniform looked up. She registered vague interest at their arrival, then seeing Zoe, announced.

'No animals in here, please.'

'But we had to bring the dog. We can't leave her in the truck. She will get too hot. We've come a long way from my farm.'

'Okay, tell me your business first then take the dog outside.'

'It's about Josie here, my cousin. Everyone thinks she is missing. It's been on the TV. But she has been with me for weeks now. I didn't know she was missing, you see, I thought she was visiting.'

Josie was grateful that Rob had taken charge. She just stood there like a silent observer as if this Josie person was some stranger.

'That's you, is it Ma'am?' the woman asked.

'Uh, oh, yes. I'm Josie. I'd...didn't know people were looking for me. I'm sorry. I w..was upset and j..just drove here to Inverell to my cousin,' she stammered.

'What is your name please and address?'

'Josie Svela, 55 Flame tree Court, Buderim.'

'When did you go missing?'

'I don't know. I was upset. I'm not sure. Last month sometime.'

'Wait over there please. I'll get someone to attend to this matter.'

The woman seemed to have forgotten Zoe and the animal rules.

They sat opposite the counter on a hard bench. Josie gazed out the window. Zoe whimpered. Rob watched his boots.

The minutes passed in tense silence. Zoe crawled in under the bench and hid behind their legs as if she knew she was not welcome. Just as well she stayed invisible as a large broad blue uniformed man emerged from within the station and came to stand before them. Rob and Josie stood, and Zoe huddled further beneath the bench, tangling herself in the loops of farm rope.

'So, you are Josie Svela, the missing woman from the Sunshine Coast?' he asked in a booming voice proportionate to his size.

'Yes, that's me,' Josie replied in a tiny, strained voice echoing her discomfort.

'What's that? Can't hear you.'

'I said, yes, I'm Josie Svela. I'm the woman in the hamster shirt on the news. See, I'm wearing the shirt.'

'Can I see some identification, please?'

Josie foraged in her handbag and produced her driver's license from her purse. She also passed over her Medicare card.

'Okay, now we have established that. Come with me and we will take down further details.'

Josie and Rob and a tangle-footed Zoe followed the monstrous man down a hallway and into a small office. The desk was strewn with paperwork. There seemed no order to it, no piles, or folders.

'Sit!' he bellowed.

They sat. Somehow, he either did not see or decided to ignore Zoe.

'Where have you been for the last month, Mrs Svela?'

'Here in Inverell, on my cousin's farm. This is Rob Smith, my cousin.'

'Can I see your license please, sir?'

Rob obliged by passing over his ID.

'Why are you here at your cousin's?' the man asked.

'I just am. I was upset. I ran away. This seemed a good place to come to get away.'

'Away from what?'

'Away from my life.'

'But you didn't tell anyone you were running away?'

'No, I didn't tell anyone. Rob didn't even know because there's no phone or TV reception out on Macintyre Road.'

'You see, Sergeant, I thought she'd just come for a visit. My wife died not long ago,' Rob explained.

'It's Superintendent. Oh, I see. But this has made work for the police all for nothing. Do you realise it was irresponsible to worry everyone, especially your family.'

He sounded angry but then he softened. 'But it happens a lot. Missing people don't always see themselves as missing.'

'Oh, like Agatha Christie. She went missing.' Josie felt better linking herself with her favourite novelist.

The superintendent looked perplexed. If he did know who Agatha Christie was, he wasn't seeing Josie's point. He frowned and continued taking notes.

They sat in silence. Even Zoe sat quietly at their feet.

'Well, that's it. We will close the file on you and notify your family. We will tell the media as well in case they want to cover it on the news bulletin.'

That seemed it. Josie sighed with relief. It had not been as bad as expected. They were not carting her off to the cells for creating a nuisance, for wasting police time. She was free.

Outside the air seemed fresher than before, the sun brighter. The rain and clouds cleared as if life offered a new beginning.

'Let's take Zoe over to that park. She needs a walk after being cooped up in there. I need a walk too,' announced Josie.

Rob seemed in agreement as he followed her across the road. Zoe sensed a change in the mood and barked with excitement.

Rob sat at a picnic table while Josie walked Zoe. He was deep in thought and felt all the long dark months of mourning were waiting to consume him again. As soon as

Josie left, they would return with a vengeance to overshadow his days and steal his rest at night. The torture would return. Josie, bright, sweet Josie she had no idea how much her visit had helped him.

Suddenly there was a commotion of voices, raised voices and Zoe was barking. What was happening? Was Josie in danger? He rose from the bench and looked to where Josie had been at the far side of the park. She was not alone. There were two other women with her, and Zoe was barking excitedly in a happy way. Who could Josie know in Inverell?

Josie saw him standing there. She called out, 'Rob, come here!'

He marched across to the three women and was shocked to come face to face with Josie's sister, Hen.

'Rob! So good to see you. Thanks for taking care of Josie. We are so happy to see her again, and you too, of course. This is Bubbles, our friend.'

Puzzled, Rob looked from one to the other of his cousins and also took in the shapely woman who completed the trio. She had a lot of bangles on her right wrist and masses of curly long hair. He returned to face Hen.

'What are you doing here, Hen? How did you know we were here in town?'

'Bubbles and I have been playing detective. As I just told Josie, a woman in Tenterfield saw a person matching Josie's description in a yellow car with a small dog and a red pet carrier. So, we came down to investigate further and, on a hunch, I thought Josie may have come to you. I was right. And we were asking directions at the garage when I spotted Zoe, then Josie in that blessed jumper. No one has a jumper like that. So that's it. Since we've found you, I don't need directions.'

'Well done, Hen. That's amazing timing as we came to unreport Josie as a missing person. I didn't know she was missing. I thought she was just visiting. There's no TV or phone at my place. I am isolated from the world, especially since Meg...' Rob was unable to finish the sentence, but everyone understood its meaning.

'Let's have something to eat at a café. I'm suddenly starving,' announced Josie. Now things had resolved, and she wasn't going to prison, she had an appetite.

'We saw a groovy café just down the street. Let's go there,' suggested Bubbles.

She and Hen led the way, and they settled outside at a table because they had Zoe with them.

Hen launched straight into questioning her sister.

'So, have you been down here with Rob since the first night you ran away?'

'Yes, I left in the morning before Max appeared and I was here by the afternoon.'

'Ah, we were not sure if you left at night or in the day because poor Max didn't know when you went missing.' Hen replied.

'Poor Max, indeed. He was too busy with his Excita gel probably to even notice where I was. He slept in the office as usual,' Josie said with sarcasm.

The others looked at each other. Bubbles raised an eyebrow at Hen. This was a different side of the usual sweet Josie. Max did ruffle her feathers.

'Well, we are glad to see you again, Josie. But you could have told someone where you were. Not just vanish and make us all worry ourselves sick. That plus the police and media. It's been horrid for us all.'

'I'm sorry, Hen. I know. I feel really bad now about it but at the time I just had to get away and I didn't feel like talking to anyone about it. Really, I think it's sort of like when Agatha Christie vanished. She didn't tell a soul either. Police looked everywhere for her.'

'Well, where was she? At her cousin's too?' asked Bubbles.

'No, she was staying at a hotel under the name of her husband's mistress. Interesting, hey? But I think someone noticed her in the end because she was a novelist then already. She'd been upset about her mother dying and her husband running off with his secretary.'

'Quite rightly, as you would be,' commented Hen.

Rob had been silent. But he suddenly joined the conversation.

'I didn't know Josie was missing, honestly. There is no mobile reception at home and for the last year no landline phone either, because of the flood after the drought. But I did enjoy her being here. We had a great time, just like old times, wasn't it, Josie?'

'Yes, it's been marvellous. Rob's been marvellous. I even met the ghost.'

'Well, it's great you have had a marvellous time, while we have been worried sick. Honestly, Josie!' Hen gave her sister one of her more severe looks.

The coffee and toasted sandwiches arrived, and they fell silent as they ate. As Rob swilled the last of his coffee, he announced,' You must all come to the farm tonight and after a good night's sleep you can decide what to do. You are welcome to stay.'

'Okay. That would be good. Thanks, Rob. I haven't been to your farm for years. But, tomorrow, We must get Josie home. She has to face the music with Max and sort things out. Plus, Bubbles has work on Monday. Tanya wanted to come initially but it was too hard with the salon. She would have had to juggle her appointments and that is a lot of work.'

Hen was definite and Josie knew her sister was right. She had to 'face the music' and her responsibilities.

'You have to ring Tash and Aiden. Tell them you are alright. You'll have to do that before we leave town while there is reception.'

Josie nodded. Her sister was right again. Josie excused herself and went outside to ring her children. Neither answered their phones as usual so she left voicemail messages telling them she was okay and had been actually okay the whole time. She hoped they would not be angry at her like Hen.

'All done,' she announced re-joining the group.

'That was quick,' commented Bubbles.

'They didn't answer. They never do. I just left messages.'

'Okay. Then I've paid, so we're all good to go. We'll follow Rob. Are you riding with Rob or us?'

'I'll stay with Rob because of Zoe. You won't want Zoe in your posh car.'

This was true, Hen silently conceded.

Josie felt relieved. She needed to collect her thoughts not be chastised by Hen.

Bubbles and Hen followed Rob's truck out of town. When they reached the bumpy dirt road, Josie smiled at the thought of her sister in her lovely clean Lexus.

'Oh, Hen won't be enjoying the road,'

Rob laughed. 'No, I can imagine. It's not a road for city slickers.'

That night Rob made a campfire and barbequed sausages. He made his signature billy tea and a scone damper. It was delicious with butter and perfect with the sausages and tomato sauce.

Bubbles and Hen looked out of place in their city clothes. Rob was sure they had never eaten bush food like this out under the stars. The atmosphere was not the same as when it was just him and Josie. He felt sad their time together had come to an end. In the morning she would drive back in convoy with her sister and friend. Josie felt sad too. If Zoe knew her farm time was ending, she would have been sad too.

The next morning, Rob farewelled his overnight guests and Josie, his long-term visitor. Hen and Bubbles were happy to leave the farm and return home and sat in the car waiting while Josie prolonged the inevitable parting from Rob.

'Come back any time, now Josie. You are always welcome. But remember to tell people you are coming next time.'

'Sure. I will. Thanks a million, Rob. It was great staying here. Zoe and I loved our visit.'

'Now, have you got everything? Have you got the little guinea pigs tucked in the back there?'

He peered in to make sure the red carrier was settled on the back seat.

'Well, I have to go. The girls are waiting. They will follow me home. At least as far as Kilcoy. Then they know their way.'

She hugged her cousin and hopped into the driver's seat of her car. Zoe sat next to her, buckled in with her doggy seat belt.

'We're off, Zoe. Back home.'

# CHAPTER TWENTY-FIVE

## Sparkles and Spangles

'Since we are all back together again, we need to celebrate,' announced Bubbles. 'It's my fiftieth birthday next week so I'm starting early with the parties. There will be a proper party at Mum's. My sister is throwing it, but this Friday, there's a terrific raffle and prizes at the club. Let's all go. It will be a blast.'

Bubbles loved parties and celebrations. She was always looking for excuses to have one. How could we deny her, seeing it was her birthday week?

The 'club' was the local yacht club, located at Mooloolabah by the canal ways and opposite the beach. It is a two-story wooden building with some residual atmosphere from the days in the sixties when Mooloolabah was a sleepy little coastal place. The clientele and menu had moved upmarket some years ago when the coast began to boom, flooded by interstate visitors and Brisbane residents coming for the weekend. Brisbane is only a bit more than an hour away and has no real ocean beach, so residents come north and treat the Sunshine Coast as their playground.

We gathered at 5pm on the outside deck of the club which overlooked the calm waters of the saltwater canal. Cruise boats, launches and sailing boats passed by returning from a day out. Those onboard waved at us. It was customary. Something about 'boaties,' they always waved, whether to be noticed on their fine crafts or just because being at sea made them happy. We waved back.

Bubbles was rather late. It was 5.20pm, but it didn't matter. Everyone was chatting and happy, some already onto their second drinks. Demi and Dale laughed with Lorraine and Josie, work pals from Aqua Tropicana chatted amongst themselves and some others, I didn't know sat perched on high stools, deep in conversation by the deck rail. Max had declined his invitation.

I stood, feeling awkward, with Vidisha and Vinni. Normally, I would have been right into the celebratory spirit and well into my second wine, but the presence of my new Indian friends made me aware of my usual brash and at times, alcoholic habits. The serene politeness of Vidisha and Vinni impressed me. I wished I could be more like them, have some of their beauty and grace.

The lunch at their house had been amazing, the food, the customs and of course the colours (I was right into colours now) had impressed me. I envied the culture and history of their homeland. Australia, being such a new country, distinctly lacked culture and history unless you included its colonial penal settlements and the massacre of the Indigenous people. Not the proudest of histories. But I suppose every country had either a colonial or invasion past. Ours was just more recent.

'Bubbles will be here soon,' I told Vidisha, just for something to say. Vinni made me nervous. I seemed to lose my power of speech in his presence.

And sure enough, she was. Bubbles arrived on the arm of handsome Brad who had spiffed up in white shirt and Levi's. She wore a spangly sort of very short black dress that reflected the light in a flashy sort of way. What an entrance! I noted Vinni's look of surprise. Women probably did not dress like that in Gujarat. Certainly not in such a short dress anyhow. Spangles may be more common. After all, India is a vibrant, colourful country.

Bubbles livened up the gathering as she does. It suddenly felt more like a party. She circulated, showering kisses onto cheeks and hugging. Vinni found himself caught up in Bubbles' demonstrative greeting. His face flushed despite his natural tan. I grinned across at Vidisha. She was feeling her brother's discomfit.

'He is not used to this. We are not so, how do you say, open with strangers at home,' she whispered to me.

I nodded. Bubbles could be overwhelming for Aussies too. Just wait till she's had a few drinks, I thought.

The night progressed. We moved inside to our reserved table and ordered our meals. I sat between Vidisha and Vinni and was very aware that my knee kept bumping his leg or was it the other way around? Oh dear, it would be a long night!

The club and especially our table became more and more raucous. It was impossible to have a quiet conversation. I sensed Vinni's discomfit. But he said nothing. He silently ate and drank his lime and soda, ever polite and serene. I followed suit and quietly ate my crumbed fish and salad beside him. Vidisha was chatting with Demi next to her. Somehow, despite the background noise, they could hear each other.

Then the microphone squealed, and a club official announced the raffles would begin. We had all bought tickets on arrival. I had shouted our Indian guests five each, so they could experience the Aussie club culture. I'm sure they were already hating it. But it was too late now. The show had to go on. It was Bubbles' night.

The club official, now wearing a black bowler hat for some reason, started to call the winning tickets and announce the prizes. Over the general noise of chatter and laughter it was a bit difficult to follow the sequence. Numbers, names, and prizes seemed to roll into one. I was not paying much attention because I rarely won at anything especially chance things like raffles. Demi was keeping an eye out for Vidisha and Vinni's tickets. She had them laid out in front of her.

The prizes were good. Appliances, meat and fruit platters, alcohol, meal vouchers and tickets to the nearby Underwater World Aquarium where my friend Sammy, the seal lived. I chuckled and thought of Sean suddenly, wondering how he was going with his park bench lady.

Vinni looked over at me, sensing my humour. His dark eyes met mine. They were superior to both Sean's and Sammy's. I loved Vinni's dark eyes. They were, I decided, 'smoldering.' Yes, that was the right word. I smiled at Vinni. He smiled back. Heaven.

Lost in my ecstatic dreaminess at the nearness of Vinni, I awoke with a jolt as Bubbles screamed, 'Yes!' nearby.

Our whole table looked on in silence as Bubbles rose from her seat, threw her arms in the air, gestured air kisses to everyone, then swanned her way towards the stage. She strutted her stuff with much ceremony and acknowledgement all the long way across the restaurant. I'm sure she wiggled her derriere more than usual or was it just that the dress was so short? I surmised that her ticket number was the reason. Bubbles must have won a prize. I had been lost in Vinni's eyes. I didn't really care about the prizes.

But I followed my friend's public parade to the stage. The man in the bowler hat called a number at her. Bubbles checked her ticket. The man shook his head. What was happening? Had she dropped her ticket on the way, had she heard wrongly?

Demi whispered to us that Bubbles had heard her name called. She heard the man call out 'Belinda', her real name, the name on the ticket. As we watched the situation unfold, we suddenly understood and felt embarrassed for Bubbles, our friend.

'Blender. The prize is a Sunbeam blender, and it goes to Judy with ticket D53! Congratulations, Judy. A wonderful prize. Happy blending, Judy.'

Alone and empty handed on the stage, Bubbles seemed to lose her sparkle and shrink in size. She slunk back down the steps from the stage and hurried back to our table. If the lights had not been so dimmed, I'm sure her face would have glowed red. Poor Bubbles. As she sat again, she explained, 'I thought he said Belinda, but he said Blender.' An easy mistake to make with the noise and a few drinks.

As we recovered from the false alarm and our birthday girl's embarrassment, Demi suddenly piped up, 'Vinni, you've won!'

Vinni straightened in his seat with surprise.

'Go on Vinni, take your ticket. Go and collect your prize!' she urged.

I made room for Vinni to squeeze out of his seat. He rose and with our encouraging chorus of 'Go Vinni!' he set off on the journey to the stage. There was no misunderstanding this time. Vinni returned five minutes later beaming his toothpaste smile. He'd won a wonderful fruit platter, a perfect prize for vegetarian Vinni. Apart from the culture shock of an Aussie club night, it had been a good night after all.

# CHAPTER TWENTY-SIX

## In the red and feeling blue

I thought Josie's return would re-unite her with Max and their life together would now take a turn for the better. But how wrong I was. Josie's running away had been a cry for help. She'd made a statement, 'I've had enough. I can't cope.' But Max did not see it that way. He was angry and embarrassed by her actions. It had put the spotlight on their relationship. I had seen a softer, caring side of Max the day I had visited him, but Max apparently did not embrace this side very often.

Despite couples counselling at The Neighbourhood Centre, Max could not forgive Josie. As we sipped coffee at The Corner Store, Josie explained. 'It's his vanity, that darned peacock male vanity of his. Max cannot look past the fact that I left him, and it became public, even though it reflects on *my* inability to cope. I'm the nutty wife who ran away and didn't have the courtesy to tell anyone. But Max thinks everyone is laughing at him for not knowing where his wife was and also maybe for having a fruitcake wife.'

'You are not a fruitcake, Josie. He is the weird one. All those stupid schemes, all the ridiculous waste of money. Most women would object to that, maybe any woman. I know Sean's spending made me angry and that was minor compared to Max's. The main thing, as the counsellor said, is that Max never consulted you about what he did with money. That is not working as a team as marriage should be. That's financial abuse, another form of domestic abuse. Men can't just do what they want and expect us to tow the line, sanction everything.'

I felt angry for Josie and infuriated with men in general. How dare they just take over. I excepted Vinni from my universal anger at men. Vinni would not behave like that. I knew this in my heart, even though his culture was foreign to me. Vinni was a good, kind man and surely would be sensible with money. I realised that I really knew so little about the man, yet felt I knew him so well. Crazy. Maybe I was the fruitcake.

'It's not going to work, Tan. There's nothing left. Max has gambled away our savings, our house. We are in debt. Well, he is in debt, and I am too, by default. He is going to declare bankruptcy because he owes more than we have. I had no idea it was so bad. The house is totally mortgaged with the bank, and we pay interest only now and he owes money to the council, the electricity and two friends who are no longer friends because he owes them. Plus, his Visa card, Amex and American Express are at their maximum limit. There's nothing left in the bank and no income. Oh, how could it come to this? What will we do?' Josie's voice rose to a wail.

'Oh, dear. It is bad. Have you any money of your own? Can you get some from your mum?'

'No, all the money I had when I married, even my super, Max has accessed and used, and I can't inherit until Mum passes. It could be years.'

'Your super? How did he access your super?'

'I'm not sure. Perhaps years ago, when the children were young. He had a friend who was a financial adviser. They were thick as thieves. He often came to the house or Max went to his business. Something about consolidation of assets, I think. They both used to talk down to me, tell me I wouldn't understand such matters. Often a signature was required. Possibly that is how I transferred my super over into a joint fund. Max had no super from salary as he never worked for anyone, but I had the hospital super, at least $20,000.'

'Oh, I see.' It was no use now, stating the obvious, that Josie should have kept an eye on her super or put a nest egg away. Hindsight of course, is a wonderful thing. The goose was cooked as they say.

'The house is up for sale by the bank. Max says that it will sell at whatever price on the day, we have no say on acceptance value.'

Josie looked miserable. I felt powerless to help. There must be some way to help.

Finally, after a silence, I said,' You can come stay with me for a while, you know, if it is too difficult there with Max. If you need money, I can help you.'

'Thanks, Tan but until the house sells, I will stay there, sort through stuff. I sleep in the spare room, Tash's room. I don't know where he sleeps. Possibly in the main bed, sometimes in the office, his cave. The house is a mess. I don't do any housework. I don't eat or cook. Poor Zoe, she knows things are bad. She is looking thin and miserable too.'

I looked down at Zoe who lay on the grass at Josie's feet. She looked up at the mention of her name. She did not look as happy as usual. No wags of the tail, no doggy smile. Her little brown eyes, normally full of mischief, now reflected her mistress's misery. Poor Zoe.

'Oh, dear,' I said again. 'Zoe does look sad. Let me come around and help you, bring some food. Lately, I've been experimenting with Indian food, since I have become friends with Vidisha and Vinni. Their cooking is amazing. It inspires me to eat and cook Indian.'

'Yes, Indian food is yummy and it's one cuisine I've never really tried to cook. You need so many ingredients, though, all those spices. I'll try some of your cooking. Why not. I will come to you. The atmosphere at ours is toxic.'

'Okay. Come around tomorrow night about six.'

'Great, thanks, Tan. It will be good to get away from the house and to try your Indian cooking.'

'You can bring Zoe, remember. I will have something for her to eat, too.'

'Oh, you are the best! See you then.'

I walked back up the hill to my salon, leaving Josie at our outside table, chatting with Lorraine. I pondered Josie's situation as I worked that afternoon. It gave me something new to ponder, a change from pondering my feelings about Vinni. I had seen him quite a lot lately, with and without Vidisha. He had popped into the salon in the afternoons and I had asked them both to my house for lunch one Sunday.

They loved my home. I could tell their genuine interest in the garden, my vegetable patch, and the fish tanks. They were even lucky enough to meet Leroy, the garden lizard. As we went back upstairs from the garden, I warned them of my culinary abilities.

'Now don't expect a fancy feast like your Thali one. I am a simple cook.'

I had worried all week what to cook but finally admitted I was no chef and settled on simple but quality fare. I made a slow cook pot of coconut vegetable curry, cooked a pot of rice, and made chickpea flour roti. As side dishes, I added sliced banana with shredded coconut, sliced cucumber, and yoghurt.

'This is very nice, Tanya. The roti are excellent. I must try with the chickpea flour. They are nicer than wheat and millet ones.'

'Thank you. I'm happy you like it all. It's the best I can do. It's Aussie style Indian.'

'But it's perfect, Tanya,' said Vinni.

'You are too kind,' I replied.

So, the lunch had been a success. Now, we had visited each other's houses, the friendship felt stronger.

I decided to repeat the menu of that lunch for Josie's visit the next day. The only change would be adding chicken to the curry. I knew Josie liked Indian as we had been to an Indian restaurant for one of our girlfriend catch-ups.

I could tell by her face as she came through my door that she was still struggling with the situation. Even Zoe was not her usual frisky doggy self. It was understandable. A marriage drama is enough for anyone without bankruptcy thrown in too. But being Josie, she tried to be upbeat.

We opened the wine she had bought. I had told her not to 'bring a thing' but she was I guess too proud to not contribute.

As if reading my mind, she volunteered, 'Hen sent it along for us.'

I smiled and took a sip. It was good quality. Hen had money and excellent taste. We sat on the sofa, Zoe at our feet.

'So, tell me all about your new friends, Tan. You seem to be seeing a fair bit of them.'

'Yes, they are special people. I enjoy their company,' I said coolly. I wasn't sure if I should tell Josie about my feelings. It may not be a good time to share feeling happy when she was so sad. I let her lead the conversation rather than say the wrong thing. Her situation was rather delicate.

'I'll stay with Hen for a while once the house sells. She is arranging a bit of an advance on my inheritance seeing as I need it now, rather than later. But if things don't improve and I don't see how they can, I will need it from now on. You see, Hen has power of attorney since Dad died.'

'Oh, well, that will help you. Maybe you can do some extra tutoring? And you know, you can always stay here for a break from Hen's. I'm at work six days, so you won't be in the way at all. It could be fun, hey?'

'Thanks, Tan. Maybe, for a break. Hen might get sick of me, moping about. And unlike you, she is always home. Rob said I can stay anytime, too. So, really, it could be worse. At least I have places to go not like poor Max.'

'Yes, where is he now?'

'Just staying with a friend but it's one of the friends he owes money to, so not sure how long that will work.'

'Oh, dear. That's a worry. Has Max declared bankruptcy yet?'

'Yes, he had to. Otherwise, all the creditors would chase him. Already they were ringing every day. The council even sent a guy to our door. I answered it in my pyjamas. I can't believe this is happening to us. It's like in the old days when the bailiff came calling. Maybe I have to declare bankruptcy too, otherwise they will claim my inheritance when I get it and they will be chasing me too. After all, my name is on all the paperwork. Good old Max made me equal shares in everything, so I am just as liable as him for the debt.'

'Oh, Josie, that's terrible. How scary. Let me know if you need someone to go to the lawyers with you.'

'We can't afford lawyers that's a problem, too. Bankruptcy is something you file for. It doesn't cost because people have no money at this point. But it makes me sick just thinking of having to file for it too. I had no part in all the mess, except by allowing it to happen under my nose. I'm bankrupt by default. Apparently, that is the term. I went to free legal aid, and they told me that. But Max would never listen to me, concede that I had a right to how our money was spent. Somehow, he thought our joint money was his to play with. I wish I'd never allowed a joint account. I wish I'd kept my money separate.'

Josie's voice rose to a crescendo. Zoe who had slept through the whole conversation, now leapt up from the mat and stared up at her mistress. She held her head on one side in a quizzical manner. If dogs could talk, she would be saying, 'What's wrong, Mum? Don't be sad.'

Josie stifled a sob and as she looked down, noticed Zoe.

'Oh, and poor Zoe, she is so unhappy. She refuses to eat and is getting thin.

'Come on, let's eat. Zoe must be hungry. I am. The table's set. I'll serve the curry into bowls, and you can add the rest from the dishes on the table.'

I ladled the steaming curry into my favourite blue pottery bowls and carried our meal to the table. There was a bowl of chicken scraps for Zoe which I placed by her on the floor. We topped up our wines and tucked into my Indian feast. Zoe wasted no time either. She gobbled hungrily at the chicken. Her appetite had returned.

Josie liked my food though her appetite was not as hearty as usual. After hearing her sad news, I probably ate less too. We could not eat all the food before us. But I raised my glass to dear Josie.

'To better days, Josie! After darkness comes the light. After winter comes the spring.'

'Thanks, Tan. I will try to be positive. Things can't get worse,' she replied with a wan smile.

# CHAPTER TWENTY-SEVEN

## Sunshine at the Zoo

'Wow!' said Vinni. He had adopted my word. Probably because I said it so much. The way he said it always made me smile. His 'Wow' had such an element of man-child wonder.

He gazed up at the Glass House Mountains. I stopped the car so he could take a photo. Vidisha took one too, just with her phone. Vinni however had a small instamatic.

'These mountains are actually volcanic plugs left after surrounding ground, softer earth eroded away. That is why they are so steep. Captain Cook called them The Glass House Mountains because they glittered like glass as he saw them from his ship. He was sailing past, not climbing them. He was a sailor after all,' I told him.

'Yes, very good. I have heard of this Captain Cook. A great explorer in the South Seas,' Vinni replied.

I nodded. 'People climb these mountains. There are tracks up the sides. But it is dangerous and only advisable for experienced climbers. I rattled off the names of the cluster of mountains, quite long Indigenous names which I could see impressed Vinni. He took another photo with Vidisha and I, and we hopped back in the car.

We were on our way to the Australia Zoo, nearby in Beerwah, south of the coast. The late Steve Irwin and his wife, Terri had established it in the 1990's. Originally, it was a small reptile park started by Steve's father, Bob Irwin. Plenty of available land around the site and the passionate vision of Terri and Steve transformed it into an international tourist attraction.

Now, at the zoo, as well as reptiles there were all sorts of animals like otters, rhinos, lions and even a giraffe. The warm climate of the Sunshine Coast provides an excellent environment for African animals. My friends knew of the Crocodile Hunter. His fame was worldwide. The world had mourned his death from a sting ray dart in 2006. He had been making an underwater film at the time.

The zoo was, and still is, an amazing success story. Steve's children Bindi and Robert, now adults, continue their father's legacy along with Terri.

The landscape and diversity of animals, now 1200 in number, had grown since my last visit. It was a while ago, now, just shortly after Steve's tragic death. I remembered signing the huge condolence book at the front gates that day. I sighed at the passing of time and putting my nostalgia aside, concentrated on showing my new friends around.

We examined the map provided and decided on a plan of attack. It was essential as the zoo covered a vast area of 700 acres. I remember how tiring it was last time and now it was even bigger. There was so much to see.

The Australian animals were a priority for anyone who had not seen them up close, but these enclosures were on the far side of the zoo along with the African animals. So, we started at the otters. I love watching the otters. They are cheeky energetic animals so very entertaining as a starting point. It was feeding time, so we stayed to watch the creatures dive for their fish and swim along on their backs eating their meal.

'Sashim would love the otters,' Vinni said to Vidisha.
She nodded and smiled.

Who was Sashim? I kept the question to myself. It may be rude to ask. Let them tell me. Instead, I said, 'The babies are adorable as all baby animals are. So much cuter than baby humans in my opinion.'

I wasn't sure what Vinni's quizzical look my way meant. He had not given me that sort of look before.

Undeterred, I led them next to the turtles and tortoises.

'There was a very old tortoise here for years. Her name was Harriet. She was a giant Galapagos tortoise collected from the islands in would you believe 1835 by Charles Darwin, himself,' I told them.

'Really, that is amazing,' Vinni commented.

'Yes, Harriet lived in England for a few years, but it was not ideal, being too cold. Darwin's friend brought her to Brisbane and for a hundred years or so she lived in The Botanical Gardens there.'

'A hundred years!' said Vidisha.

'Wow!' said Vinni. I wonder where he learnt that expression.

Vidisha and I laughed at Vinni saying 'Wow.' Then I continued my story because I loved the story of Harriet.,

'It was years later that someone discovered Harry, the tortoise was a female. So, the name became Harriet. All her life up till then, she had been known as Harry. For the last twenty years of her life, she lived like a queen here at the zoo, being fed only the best and adored by everyone. Her favourite food was hibiscus flowers. Sadly, she died the same year that Steve did. She was 175 years old.'

'Wow!' said Vinni again.

Nearby were the signature animals of the zoo, the crocodiles, the foundation creatures of the zoo. I expected my friends to be fascinated but they seemed scared. Crocodiles were not their thing. So, we appreciated their size and snappiness and passed them and the huge Crocoseum by, to reach the Australian and African exhibits. Along the way, for it was a fair distance, we munched on crackers and sipped from our water bottles. Fortunately, it was not summer. I would never suggest a zoo trip in summer.

Vidisha and Vinni loved the kangaroos and their smaller relatives, the wallabies. 'Nowhere else in the world are there such strange animals as ours', I told them, sounding like a tourist guide. 'Isolated from the rest of the world's land mass, Australian animals developed uniquely. The mammals have pouches and feed their animals milk. The animals are tiny at birth and must claw their way into the pouch where they stay snug and warm and grow. Eventually they pop out to see the world but mostly enjoy the free ride around. Sort of like kids in a stroller.'

'Sashim liked his stroller,' commented Vinni.

Who was Sashim? I wondered again.

No explanation forthcoming, we continued past a spiny echidna, to the koala enclosure, always a hit with foreign visitors. I took a photo of them each holding a koala. They looked so happy to meet one. Personally, I find koalas cute but rather smelly, so I declined a cuddle.

'Here are the wombats, our sturdiest marsupial, maybe our grumpiest too. Because wombats resemble an anvil, a huge block of steel, you don't want to anger one by getting too close to their burrow or taking one of their babies. Appreciate wombats but give them a wide berth,'

Vinni laughed. 'Yes, they are very fat and can't move fast.'

'They can when they are angry,' I told him.

We stopped for tea at a café and spent another hour wandering the zoo, before declaring ourselves exhausted.

It had been fun. I was getting to know my friends more. But who was Sashim?

# CHAPTER TWENTY-EIGHT

## Dark Times

The bank sold Josie's house and transferred the funds to the mortgage payout. Because of a stagnant property market and the unmaintained state of the house, there were not enough funds to cover the mortgage value. This left Josie and Max penniless and in debt, an unthinkable situation considering the money they once had twenty years earlier.

Josie was distraught as expected in such a situation. Hen took her sister in at her house. Max however had nowhere to go. His parents were deceased, and he had not talked to his sister in twenty years. The news that they had fallen out over money did not surprise any of us. He remained at a friend's in exchange for doing the housework. I couldn't see that lasting long. I'd seen Max's idea of housework.

We were back at The Corner Store having coffee outside at the table Lorraine now called 'Josie's table' because she was there every day now. After walking Zoe, she came here to avoid returning to the house and Max. I had a break between bookings and had walked down the street from the salon. A coffee and cake would do us both good.

No-one had any idea of my inner anguish over Vinni, and I wanted to keep it that way. Surely in time my schoolgirl crush would shatter, and I would return to my normal adult self. So, no need to bother others. Josie must be the focus. She was far more needy of consolation. And so, it seemed was little Zoe.

'Oh, and poor Zoe, she has been so unsettled. She refuses to eat and has rejected her bed because it's in the laundry. She is used to sleeping beside my bed on the floor. But Hen and Jim have never had animals and won't have them in the house, so it's difficult. Jim is even fussing about the guinea pigs. He's worried they will ruin his lawn.'

'Oh, I see. That's tough. Well, maybe you should come stay with me. The offer is always open. I'd love Zoe and you to come stay. But I might have to fix a fence for the backyard, so Zoe won't escape.'

I wondered if Vinni was handy with fences. *STOP! Stop thinking about Vinni. Enough. Josie is the focus.*

'I'll see how we go. Hen has been marvellous, really. What can I expect, anyhow? I'm a homeless over fifty woman with a useless husband and an anxious dog. I must make the best of things,' she replied. Josie was trying her best to be positive and upbeat. I admired her for it.

# CHAPTER TWENTY-NINE

## Pastels at Wisteria

Wisteria Park was the perfect spot for an informal wedding. Demi and Dale both looked like springtime maidens in their long pastel dresses. Demi wore blue and Dale lemon. Lorraine had woven flowers into garlands for their hair. We were all there, her friends, as the celebrant pronounced them 'partners for life!' It rhymed nicely with the more traditional 'man and wife.' Lorraine and I exchanged a smile. The world had changed in our lifetime. Two women could now marry legally.

We all wished them further happiness. They were already happy, happier than most man and wife couples. Certainly, this all-girl couple had already lasted longer than Sean and I had. And their wedding was no fuss, inexpensive and joyous. Sean and I had wasted precious funds on a formal sit-down wedding reception. Just a simple afternoon tea and drinks in the park, Demi and Dale had the right idea. The brief ceremony over, the girls sealed their commitment and love with a kiss. Then the unexpected happened.

Demi threw her bouquet over her shoulder, and it hit me on the head. But I caught it, which technically as the old tradition goes, suggests that I would be next to marry. What a laugh! And everyone laughed so I had to laugh too.

'Go, Tanya! When's the wedding?' Bubbles cried.

I blushed. If I was not so lovestruck, I like the others would think nothing of this. I clasped the small posy. Could I hope for love again at my age? Vinni arrived carrying two glasses of punch. I blushed again.

'So, you are a good catch. You have the flowers,' he said,

He passed me a glass of punch. Did he realise the double meaning of 'a good catch'? He certainly would be a 'good catch' but was I? Twenty years ago, maybe, but now? Did Vinni stay by my side the rest of the afternoon because he was shy? I was aware of a few curious glances our way. Vinni seemed relaxed in my company, away from his sister. Vidisha was chatting with the photographer. He wanted her in the wedding photos. She looked so beautiful in her crimson sari and was the best and most colourfully dressed of all of us.

'The flowers match your dress, Tanya. They are very pretty. You are very pretty too,' Vinni announced.

I blushed. 'Thank you, Vinni. That is very sweet of you. Since I met your sister, I wear more colour. I love colour now.'

'Your green dress matches your eyes. You have lovely eyes, Tanya. I have never seen eyes of green before.'

I blushed again. 'Oh, thank you, Vinni. You have beautiful brown eyes.'

We remained locked in each other's eyes until Lorraine came to say hello.

'Now, you must introduce me to your very handsome friend, Tanya.'

'Oh, hi Lorraine. This is Vinni, Vidisha's brother.'

'What a splendid pair you are. Both as beautiful as each other. I do love Vidisha's sari. It adds such colour to the occasion.'

I gathered the 'beautiful pair' meant Vinni and Vidisha, not sadly Vinni and me.

That would be too much to ask. Vinni and I as a pair. But it was okay to dream.

ﾋﾟ

A wedding, then a funeral some weeks later. Edith finally died at Twilight Time. She choked on a toffee, well two, actually. She was a greedy woman. I nearly said 'she came to a sticky end' when Josie told me but bit my tongue. Maybe Josie did deep down have some feelings for her mother. However, I thought otherwise when she and Hen told me how they sprinkled Edith and Arthur's ashes.

The two sisters stood by the river. Josie held the green urn. She opened it and gathered a handful of ashes and threw them to the wind. She repeated this then passed the urn to her sister who performed the same actions.

'Goodbye, darling Dad! Be at peace, Arthur.'

From the other urn they repeated the procedure but threw the ashes in the opposite direction. Then unceremoniously, Hen dumped the rest on the beach and stomped on them. No blessing, no good-bye It was over. They were free of Edith. So was Arthur.

# CHAPTER THIRTY

## Colours of Christmas

Before we knew it, Christmas was on the horizon. Shop windows filled with tinsel and decorations shouted 'CHRISTMAS SALE' and it was difficult to avoid the December madness. Everyone wanted to look their best, so my salon bookings filled early.

Clients asked, 'What are you doing for Christmas, Tanya?'

I had no answer. It seemed miserable to tell the truth, to say, 'Somehow, I'll survive it.'

I had no plans. Since Sean and I had split, my Christmas depended on invitations to other people's Christmases. It seemed pointless to roast a turkey just for one. I knew eventually I would host my own gathering to thank my friends for sharing their Christmases with me. I wondered what Sean would do this year. Perhaps he would celebrate with his brother again. I had been so distracted by the Josie thing and then Vinni, that I had not checked the park bench lately. Certainly, Sean had not visited the salon with his usual frequency. Maybe he had a lady friend, perhaps the one I had seen there with him a few times. I resolved to check more often.

Josie was spending Christmas with Hen and Jim, Bubbles with her family. They had all invited me. Lorraine had also invited me to The Corner Store version of Christmas. I was considering all these options when another most unexpected offer came my way.

Vinni and Vidisha were going home to India to sort out some family issues then take a holiday north to New Delhi, Jaipur and Agra. Would I like to come?

My voice spoke for me before the concept even registered.

'Wow! I'd love to come!' it said.

My friends seemed surprised but pleased for me. Josie would move into my place while I was away. She was less upset now an inheritance was imminent. Edith's passing was a relief for the sisters. No more money worries for Josie and Hen could have her house back.

'The money is in a family trust which is a blessing. It means the bank can't seize the funds. I will negotiate a settlement with the bank before the probate. So technically, I won't inherit until after the bank settlement,' Josie told me.

'Will you have enough money left?'

'Yes, there will be enough for a little house out of town, something small, with land. I want to start an animal minding business, dogs, cats, guinea pigs, maybe even birds. A house on an acre or two with a shed would be great.'

'Sounds good, Josie. I'm excited for you! A new future for you and Zoe.'

I did not dare ask about Max and where he would go with no money.

'I'm excited for you, too, Tan. Wow! A holiday in India. How marvellous. Is there something between you and the dishy Vinni? I noticed you seemed quite chummy at the wedding.'

'Well, I do like him, a lot, but I'm not sure if it is reciprocated. I mean, why would he like me?'

'Why wouldn't he, Tan? Don't be silly. You are gorgeous, too. Your eyes, your lovely figure, so slim still and you, just you, are very special. No more doubting ourselves, no more put downs. We are amazing! '

Josie was powering ahead with positivity. I was happy for her. Both our lives had changed so much since she went missing.

# CHAPTER THIRTY-ONE

## All the Colours of India

We arrived in the human chaos that is modern day Mumbai, once colonial Bombay. Nothing prepared me for the chaos, the sheer mass of people, vehicles and animals that crowded the streets. Not my previous travel in Bali, Fiji, or Singapore. I thought I was a seasoned traveler but now I knew I was not. India was a shock to the senses in every way. People, people, and more people covered the roads and walkways. Then there was the noise, a cacophony of it. Shouting, car horns, bicycle bells, motor bikes, children, industrial noise. The airport had seemed crowded enough, noisy enough.

Vinni and Vidisha sensed my shock and steered me to a taxi. As he drove through the streets, the taxi driver honked his horn. Despite the seeming chaos of the traffic, people and vehicles moved around without crashing, letting us through. I gazed on in wonder. It was like the parting of the Red Sea, of course on a lesser and drier scale.

'They are aware of everything, these drivers. They have to be. But westerners and tourists, they would crash in a moment. They rarely drive here. Best to leave it to the professionals, the taxi drivers,' Vinni told me.

We arrived at our splendid colonial style hotel. I liked it, a lot. It was gracious, old worldly, not a modern steel glass monstrosity lacking atmosphere. It had a lovely garden at the rear, around a pool. We sat and dangled our feet in the cool water and enjoyed a fruit juice cocktail. It was refreshing after the long tiring flight from Brisbane and subsequent culture shock.

The rooms were lovely. We had one each. I wasn't sure whether Vidisha had booked two or three. I had paid my share of the travel expenses but had not questioned her bookings. They knew India, I did not.

The next afternoon we flew to their hometown, Surat. It was a pleasant two-hour flight. After Mumbai, Surat seemed provincial, less chaotic but still busy as India is, and must always have been. So many people massed together can't be anything but busy.

Surat is a city of the Gujarat province in Western India, a fast-growing city, Vinni told me because of textiles and diamond polishing. Vinni's family had a cotton mill here that sadly burned down three years ago. Vidisha said it was the reason they left for Australia. A new start, an attempt to forget. But had it worked? Here they were back again. To see their family, to start again?

I did not know and felt reluctant to ask. I sensed sadness in their past. I hoped in time, they would tell me more.

We caught a taxi from the airport and arrived at an address across the city. It was a low-lying area, mostly residential amongst shops and restaurants. The street bustled with cars, buses, and bikes, but less so than the city centre and Mumbai.

My friends gestured me in through the green wooden door of the house. Two older women and a man greeted us. A young boy stood behind them. Vinni rushed over to scoop him into his arms. The boy laughed. As he put his arms around Vinni's neck, I noticed the boy had a badly scarred forearm.

The flurry of exchanged hugs and kisses continued until Vidisha stood back and introduced me to her parents, aunt and Vinni's son, Sashim. This was a shock. I had no idea Vinni had a child. But the name was familiar. I had heard Vinni and Vidisha mention the name Sashim the day we visited the zoo. Where then was Vinni's wife, the mother? The family, unaware of my shock, smiled and quaintly bowed, chatting and laughing the whole time, looking from one to another.

Vidisha showed me to a room, a lovely room, overlooking a tiny garden courtyard. The sun streamed in across the small but adequate space. I unpacked my bag. We were here for a week. Then, trying to hide my shock, I joined the family in the main area of the house.

Here a splendid table was set. A huge quantity and variety of dishes awaited our appetites. Now, a little used to the cuisine, I helped myself, following the others. Rice, dahl, beans, vegetable dishes. I recognised the sweet but salt spiced flavours. We sipped fragrant black tea.

The older parents and aunt had little English so I could not follow the conversation, but it was happy. Everyone seemed happy so I tried to put aside my questions and be happy too. Vinni seemed very happy and smiled over at me during the meal. Sashim chattered on in his language. I gathered he was telling funny stories because everyone laughed each time he finished talking. I smiled at the happy family enjoying each other's company. Though I could not understand any Hindi, Vidisha translated bits for me, so I felt included.

The next morning the conversation between the family seemed more serious. I came to breakfast to find this change in tone and mood. Vidisha met my appearance with a smile as usual, but it was a sad smile. Something was wrong but I did not know what. Everything had been happy last night.

Only later was I able to question Vidisha and then I had to take care not to be nosy. It felt rude to ask questions. I was in a different culture, now.

'It is the mill. We must go and see the ruins of the mill and decide what to do with the site. Three years it has sat there. Our parents need our decision on whether to rebuild,' she told me.

But even after this explanation, I knew there was more to tell. Vinni was different. He had been crying, I'm sure of it. His wonderful brown eyes looked glazed and puffy. Could it be the anticipated visit to the ruins, his family business or was there more tragedy, unspoken pain involved?

I stayed behind that day with the aunt and young Sashim. The family all went to the ruins across the town. Sashim spoke English well as he learnt it at school. He told me all about his friends, his school but nothing of the mill and fire. I only learnt that Vidisha and Vinni had lived at the mill, behind it in another building, not here with the parents. Where was Vinni's wife? This puzzled me, and why was such a lovely woman as Vidisha not married? This seemed unusual for the culture. Everywhere you looked the families were large and all the young women had babies.

From feeling happy on arrival here, I now felt isolated and out of place like an intruder. This was a close family with a painful past and I was just an interloper, an outsider. Suddenly, panic struck, I felt the need to go home.

When my friends returned, visibly upset, I felt unable to voice my panic. Instead, I sat silent and sad at the table with them that night. No-one was eating much. I excused myself and went to my room.

I lay on the bed and closed my eyes. The sounds of the evening rushing on outside came to me through the open window. Then it grew dark, and I lay there still in the darkness. The noises of the night were the same but a little softer. Honking cars, voices, children crying, even a cow mooing somewhere nearby. Then there was a soft knock at my door, and someone called my name. It was Vidisha.

I opened the door. She came in, switched a soft light on and we sat together on the bed.

'Tanya, I need to tell you something. So, you understand,' she said.

I nodded. She continued. 'There was a fire at our mill, the Patel family mill. It had been our business for generations, our livelihood but then suddenly it was gone. But it was not just the mill, that night. Some of our family died in the fire too.'

'Oh, no, Vidisha. I am so sorry. I did not know.'

'Yes, how could you. We have not explained. But now, you need to know. You are here with us, and Vinni and I care about you.'

A tear came to my eye. I let it gather but placed my hand on Vidisha's soft brown hand. The flesh felt familiar, warm like Vinni's hand but softer and smaller.

She looked over at me. Despite the dim light, I could see tears in her eyes. They glistened and caught the lamplight. Her large brown eyes were beautiful and sad.

'My husband and Vinni's wife, they died that night along with an unborn baby, Vinni's baby.'

I could barely breathe. I gasped, held the bed frame and let out a cry of pain.

'No, oh, no, Vidisha. That is too terrible. You poor darlings! I had no idea.'

Then Vidisha wept. I held her and wept too.

# CHAPTER THIRTY-TWO

## In a Blur

The next day was a blur for me, a blur of misery. The knowledge of the terrible truth of the family tragedy made me feel even more awkward in this family home that had lost a family.

Although Vinni and Vidisha also seemed subdued and quiet, they did not neglect their manners. They greeted me as usual at the morning meal as did their family. Sashim came to sit next to me. We had bonded in a way yesterday. He had enjoyed practicing his English with me and had enjoyed showing me his collection of ship models in his room. Some of them were famous ships, like the Titanic. I had chatted about this 1912 liner and the tragedy of loss of life not realising this young boy had lost his mother and unborn sibling and had obviously been apart from his father for some time.

I felt bad about this now. But Sashim seemed unaffected and chatted away beside me explaining the food and telling me about his friend who was visiting today.

'Sandeep, my friend, has a new bike. We will go for a ride together. I hope I can keep with him. My bike is old and not so fast.'

'Oh, yes, I hope you have fun. It will be good riding. Lots of fresh air and the day is warm and sunny.'

I made conversation but my mind was elsewhere, with Vinni and Vidisha who sat opposite. My appetite deserted me. From devouring eagerly, loving every dish, I now just sat and pushed around the rice and dahl on my plate. I tried to swallow but the bolus of food caught in my throat. I gulped some tea to wash it down.

Vinni watched me as he often did. I managed a wan smile and continued sipping the tea. Its warmth helped me relax a little. The day stretched ahead. How could I get through this day? I felt awash with shock and grief, yet it was not even my family. I drew Vidisha aside.

'I think I must leave, Vidisha and fly home. Your family have been amazing. You are amazing, but you need to grieve alone not with a stranger in your midst. I had no idea of your situation. I thought it was just a holiday…'

The rest, how I really felt, I could not say. She nodded in understanding but touched my arm and replied softly.

'No, Tanya, it is not necessary. We want you here with us as our friend. You are welcome in our parent's home. They understand. And Vinni needs you. He has been better since you came into his life. Please stay. Later we will go see Agra and Jaipur. It will be a holiday. Sashim will come too. I can tell he likes you.'

So, I stayed, and things felt better. Christmas here was a small celebration, unlike any other Christmas I'd known. There were no presents, no turkey or ham, just the usual Indian dishes. However, I think to cheer me, Vidisha made a selection of sweets. They were delicious, milky and sweet. She had wrapped them in coloured cellophane, so they added a festive element to our table.

The business of the mill seemed to resolve. Vinni and Vidisha disappeared to lawyers and builders. The mill would be rebuilt. The family business would continue. Did this mean my friends would stay in India? I did not know and did not dare to ask. My heart felt tangled in the lives of the Patel family, maybe irretrievably.

There were so many questions, still unanswered. How did Vinni, Vidisha and Sashim survive the tragedy that claimed their families? This was the main one that puzzled me. Had Vinni tried to save his family but only saved Vidisha and Sashim?

I had to trust that I would learn the answers in time. The holiday part of the trip was about to begin. I hoped this would be a healing time for my friends, a time to soften their pain.

# CHAPTER THIRTY-THREE

## The Pink City of Jaipur

The sights, the smells, I had braced myself for the experience that is India. But it is not possible to come from the orderly, quiet life of Australian suburbia into India and not be in a constant state of shock and wonder. There is so much activity, everywhere, all the time. Street vendors, beggars, children, trucks, buses, even cows clog the streets. Without Vinni and Vidisha on either side of me, I would never dare to cross the street. The teeming current of activity does not even resemble the orderly stream of cars back home. Nothing seems orderly or under control, yet Vinni assured me it is.

I could only trust in his and Vidisha's judgement on such matters. After the first few days, I started to relax into the swirl of humanity, let my heartbeat to its drum. A holiday in India, a trip of a lifetime!

Anything can happen in India. I was learning. As we travelled, I saw snake charmers with deadly cobras, men with their heads buried in the ground, still alive with legs pointing straight up to the sky. Both were common practice to earn money.

'The man with his head in the sand has a straw to breathe through. See, if you look closely, Miss Tanya.'

Sashim pointed and I could just see a tiny piece of straw emerging from the dirty sand.

Along rivers, women washed themselves and their laundry, banging the colourful fabrics on the rocks, squatting the whole time. I saw all manner of beggars, children without limbs, blind children, dirty poor children. My heart ached for India, for these children. But this, Vinni kept telling me, was India, his India and he was proud to show it to me.

From Gujarat we travelled north to Rajasthan and its capital, Jaipur, an amazing pink city set on plains surrounded by barren hills. This northwestern area of India is dry and includes part of the Thar desert which extends into nearby Pakistan. The main area of the old city has beautiful architecture.

The Jaipur palace dominates the space. We walked up the hill and wondered at its beauty and size. Vinni paid for Sashim to have an elephant ride to the palace. The boy sat proudly like a young prince on his colourfully dressed and painted elephant. He waved down at us mere pedestrians.

'The current maharaja lives here now,' Vinni told me.

'Oh! Really. I thought they all went in 1949 when Pakistan was annexed?' I had been reading my guidebook.

'Yes, some did because at independence the funding for their lifestyle disappeared. The first prime minister of the new India would not fund their palaces. There was a lot of prejudice against the maharajas as many Indians thought they sided with the British. Maharajas and their palaces were a casualty of independence. Some managed to maintain their palaces and wealth though. Many converted parts of their palace into hotels so they had an income. There are many such hotels in Rajasthan.'

'And surprise, Tanya, we are staying in one tonight,' added Vidisha.

'Oh, really! Wow! That is amazing.'

My friends laughed at my enthusiasm.

Our hotel was indeed one of these refurbished maharaja palaces. I wasn't totally sure if it was a joke, this promised palace. But no, there it stood in all its former glory, a glorious relic from the past. Inside it was just as opulent. Beautiful furniture and wall decors spoke of its illustrious past. I was in awe, speechless. Vidisha checked us in and soon a bellboy arrived to take us to our rooms.

'Oh, my room is amazing,' I gushed to Vidisha. I had rushed to hers to see if it had the same amazing view over the pink city.

'Yes, we all have a view. There is the palace where we were this morning.'

'How can we afford this place. Have I paid you enough?' I asked.

'Yes, it is all good. The hotel is only four star. It is not overly expensive, but I agree it is the real India of the past. I love it, too. My first time staying at a palace. It is a treat for us all.'

That night, we went out to a local restaurant near the palace. The curries were rather spicy, but I enjoyed everything else, especially the cool jellied tapioca that soothed my burning tongue. Sashim liked the dessert too. He had an extra serve of the jeweled pink jelly and white pearly tapioca.

As we walked back to the hotel, our palace for two nights, the pink buildings of Jaipur seemed bathed in a soft orange glow. I felt a surge of happiness at being here in Incredible India.

The next morning, we enjoyed a wonderful banquet style breakfast from which anyone in the world could eat from.

Food from all cuisines abounded. There were croissants, cereals, fruit, even bacon and eggs and then many, many types of Indian food.

'There is western food, Tanya,' Vinni informed me.

'I have a policy when I travel of eating local,' I replied. 'The Indian food is more interesting for me as long as the curries are not too hot like they were last night.'

'This one is mild. I can tell by its colour. And here is your favourite vegetable dish.'

'Yes, I do like that one. I'll just have that with rice and some fruit. That will be plenty.'

I piled the fragrant vegetables and coconut rice and helped myself to some cut fruit. Vinni served himself a huge plate of almost everything and sat silently eating besides Vidisha and I. She like me was selective, only taking her favourite dishes. Sashim, being in his growing years, tucked into a large plate of mixed food.

'This morning we will go to the main bazaar in the old city where we are now. You can buy some clothes or jewellry there. The variety and prices are good.'

'Excellent, Vidisha. It sounds great fun. Will you come shopping too, Vinni?'

'Oh, yes. Sashim and I will most certainly come. Shopping is good here.'

A man who likes shopping. Vinni never failed to impress. I grinned over at him. He smiled his delicious smile in return. I think Vidisha noticed this exchange.

Rajasthan is famed for its men who wear pastel-coloured turbans and sport large, twirled moustaches. I tried not to stare at them. The women as in most places we had been, wore colourful saris. Together a traditionally dressed Indian couple looked absolutely splendid.

The Johari bazaar or jeweler's market did not disappoint. The display captured the colour and sparkle of India. Jade, sapphire, amber, emeralds and rubies and many more stones I did not recognise graced silver and gold necklaces, rings and bangles. Overwhelmed, I surveyed the selection in awe.

'Let me buy you something, Tanya. What would you like?' offered Vinni.

'Oh, no, Vinni. You must not. Thank you though. I am not really a jewellry girl as you can see.' I held up my bare wrists and hands to illustrate.

'All the more reason why you need a souvenir from colourful Jaipur,' he said. He pointed to a gold bangle. 'This bangle is very nice. It is simple but has these lovely turquoise stones. You like turquoise, I notice.'

'Yes, I do and Vidisha told me it is one of my colours. That and soft green and bright pink. It is lovely. But I can't let you buy it, Vinni. I can pay for it.'

But before I could act, before I even knew its price, Vinni scooped the bangle up and presented it to the vendor. Vinni passed over a bundle of rupees and suddenly the bangle was mine. Vinni fastened it on my right hand and the deal was done. Astonished and flustered, I gazed down at the sparkling gift. It did suit my now tanned wrist.

'Oh, thank you, Vinni. You are too kind and generous!'

'For you, Tanya. Because you are very special.'

I blushed. If Vinni thought I was special, it was a special moment.

'It suits you,' Vidisha whispered. 'Vinni is happy to spoil you. Let him. It makes him happy.'

'It is a good bangle, Miss Tanya,' pronounced Sashim. He gave me the thumbs up signal. I laughed at this unexpected gesture.

I smiled at lovely Vidisha. 'Vinni is most kind. I will buy him something too when I see the right something.'

We left the markets and arrived at the famous Hawa Mahal, a central landmark of the old city. It is an amazing tall red-pink building with hundreds of small windows built so ladies of the royal household could privately watch processions in the city. We climbed the stairs to see the view of the streets below and the wondrous pink palace nearby. Through the crenellated window surrounds, I viewed everyday life in progress below. I indulged in a moment of fantasy, imagining myself as a royal lady overlooking the commoners. as they went about their everyday lives.

I decided that day that India is not like anywhere else. It is a magical colourful jumble of people, modern life and ancient customs. It is past and present cohabiting time in a swirl of colour.

# CHAPTER THIRTY-FOUR

## The Taj of White Marble

From Jaipur, we entered the chaos of New Delhi, a thriving non-stop city. Its intensity was rather overwhelming, similar to Mumbai. We only stayed one night. The next morning, we caught the train to Agra. I couldn't wait to see the Taj Mahal, one of the Seven Wonders of the Modern World. Although when I read it dated to the 17th century, I questioned the 'Modern' part of this description.

'The original Seven Wonders all dated from ancient times, The Hanging gardens of Babylon, The Pharos, the Colossus of Rhodes are a few I know,' Vinni said.' I read that The Sydney Opera House is one of the other Modern Wonders.'

'Really, how surprising. I just take it for granted as I remember it being built.'

'For us, it was like seeing a wonder,' Vidisha said.

'Well, nowhere as amazing as the Taj will be, I'm sure. The Taj is a monument to love. The opera house is well, just an opera house.'

'But it is unlike any other. It is a sail filled opera house, set on a magnificent harbour.'

I did concede the sight of the white concrete sails on the harbour had become a symbol of Australia as the white Taj was a symbol of India.'

⁂

'First class travel is essential. You see we have leather seats, and the carriage is clean compared to the other classes, and well, on the roof it is neither clean nor safe.'

'On the roof? People travel on the roof? Like they do on the buses?'

I had marvelled at how many people could fit in and on the buses that beeped their way through the traffic.

'Yes, of course. This is India. Anything goes. Poor people have few choices. Listen and watch, you will see and hear the roof travellers.'

And I did. Men, women and even children clambered past our windows, upwards to the roof. We could hear the clatter of their feet above us.

'They hang onto the brass rails. They are good at hanging on. Few fall,' Vinni told me. He smiled at my shocked expression. He had been smiling at me all week. How I loved him.

Suddenly there was a lot of shouting and the banging of doors. Whistles screeched. More shouting, more banging and we were off on our train adventure, off to Agra.

I remarked that some young men still clung to the sides of the train.

'The roof must be too crowded. These travellers are not safe. If a train comes the other way, they could get crushed or blown off with the force of air. They travel at their own risk.'

Vinni smiled again as I looked aghast at this information. I didn't want to witness this scenario. He sensed my concern and gently placed his broad warm hand upon mine. I loved that simple gesture. It was a small act but had a huge effect. Sashim smiled across at us from his seat opposite. He seemed happy to share his father with me, a stranger from the other side of the world. Yes, Sashim seemed a nice boy, like his father.

Vidisha whispered to me. 'Here comes our breakfast.'

A very rattly steel trolley entered our carriage. There was a lot of clatter and banging of metal dishes and utensils. I tried to see by looking over the seat.

'It will take a while to get here. But the food will be good and hot,' she told me.

'It smells amazing. All food here does. I have never eaten as many vegetables, chickpeas and rice.'

Like anywhere in Asia, rice was the dominant cereal, the staple food upon which everything else was piled in fragrant dollops. Fortunately, I love rice and vegetables and don't mind chickpeas. The breakfast was good. We chose an assortment and shared. I loved the butter fried potatoes and the hot milk chai, all served in metal containers, so they kept the heat. Everyone around us was eating. The train ran a good buffet service to feed so many.

Warmed and fed, I settled in to watch the scenery. I focused my gaze away from the men hanging to the sides just behind our window. I sat between my friends, with Vinni by the window. The twenty-first century did not seem to exist outside in the countryside. People used the fields as toilets, unashamedly baring their backsides to go about their bodily functions. I had seen this elsewhere in India. It failed to shock now. Further on, men and many women, not all young and fit-looking, worked with primitive spades and rakes. Children ran around, the older ones helping their family.

'What are they growing?' I asked. The soil looked poor and clumpy and the crops stunted.

'I think it's vegetables, maybe potatoes?'

I nodded. Root crops probably didn't need the best soil. I had even grown potatoes myself accidentally from peelings in my compost bin. Vidisha passed our plates and cutlery to the steward who returned with his trolley from the opposite direction. She briefly chatted with him in her language, Hindi.

'It is less than an hour now, to Agra,' she told us. We nodded. The train rattled on. The countryside broadened to reveal fields under cultivation.

'They are growing wheat and millet,' Vinni informed me. 'The roti and parathas we eat are made of these. Not all grain is rice.'

The labour force of India was again apparent. Men loaded a rusty cart with grain stalks. There were bullocks in some of the fields, beasts of burden helping the men who were but beasts of burden themselves. I saw no modern agricultural tools, no tractors, no harvesters, just man and beast working beside each other.

A flash of movement and colour reminded me of the train's side travellers.

'The men on the sides must get sore arms. How do they hang on for so long?'

'Sometimes, they don't. They try their best because falling is usually fatal, especially if a tiger is in the fields. The man would be instant breakfast.'

Sashim laughed but I looked in shock at Vinni. He smiled again. Was he kidding me? Could a man really fall off a moving train into a tiger's path and be eaten. Maybe. We were in India.

We arrived in Agra that afternoon, to see, Vinni said, 'The jewel of India, the symbol of India, the Taj Mahal.'

My guidebook informed me that strictly speaking the Taj Mahal is more an example of Mughal or Islamic architecture than Indian, but I did not argue the point. Every travel brochure on India featured a photo of the Taj monument. It was perhaps India's strongest drawcard for tourists. The number of travellers that exited the train at Agra bore testament to the fact. Indians flock to Agra as well as international tourists. Like the Eiffel Tower and the Tower of Pisa, everyone wants a photo in front of the Taj Mahal.

'It would be nice to have a photo without people. Just the beautiful building itself.'

'You can, Tanya. We are staying in a hotel that has a view of the Taj. You can take photos at different times. The Taj changes its colour with the time of day. Orange at sunset, blue when bathed by moonlight, pink at dawn then yellow through to brilliant white at noon.'

'Really, Vidisha?'

'Yes, really. The Taj is a chameleon, the most beautiful in the world.'

I couldn't wait to meet and see the palace in all its moods. For it is a palace as well as a tomb or mausoleum. 'mahal' means palace and Taj is a shortening of Mumtaz, the name of Shah Jahan's beloved wife buried there.

True to Vidisha's promise, our hotel room offered a not-too-distant view of the Taj. The light now soft in the afternoon, presented a pale peach coloured version of the monument. It was a beautiful sight, framed by the crenellated shutters of my hotel window. I gazed in wonder until Vidisha came to fetch me. We were going for drinks by the hotel pool before taking dinner in the restaurant.

'It is incredible and very beautiful,' I whispered to Vidisha as we left my room.

'Just wait until you see it up close, tomorrow.'

I couldn't wait. I felt excited. The whole trip so far had been amazing, part of another world far from Buderim, far from the familiarity of Australia.

We sat and enjoyed a cool drink by the pool. Sashim splashed around nearby in the pool. On request, I refreshed my friend's knowledge of the monument. My well-thumbed guidebook offered many interesting facts. We do not usually carry around guidebooks to our own country. So, I, the foreigner told my Indian born friends about their national monument.

'It is a monument to love. Shah Jahan loved his Mumtaz more than his other two wives, wife number one and wife number three, because they were political alliance marriages not marriages of love. The Shah, then a prince, became engaged to Mumtaz when they were only 14 and 15. He married wife one first before marrying Mumtaz when she was 19. Then together, they had 14 children. While in childbirth with the last, Mumtaz died. The Shah was so distraught that he isolated himself to grieve and when he emerged sometime later his hair was white, and his stature bent. He then embarked on the construction of Mumtaz's tomb. It took twenty years to build.'

'Yes, I remember parts of this story,' Vinni commented. 'It cost a fortune because of the white marble used and all the precious stones inlaid into the walls.'

'Twenty-eight types of jewels,' Vidisha added. 'Sapphire, onyx, amber, jade and ruby are just a few. All the patterns are of flowers and plants. There are no animal or human forms.'

'I wonder why. This is unusual. Most temples have human figures, gods and animals,' Vinni said.

'The guidebook does not say why. But it does say 'Every frieze had to be identical as The Taj is a monument to Mumtaz but also one to symmetry. Wherever you stand, it is symmetrical. Four minarets, a central dome make it so.'

Our drinks finished, our knowledge expanded, we left the now darkening poolside for the warmth and light of the restaurant.

After dinner in my room, I gazed out at the moonlit version of the Taj. It was so beautiful and would remain my favourite version. The moon above the monument lit the palace with a pale blue luminosity. So beautiful and so tranquil in the near distance. I pulled a chair close to the window and sat in wonder. I must have fallen asleep for a time as I woke chilled and stiff. The moon had vanished somewhere else in its orbit of the earth. The Taj was only just visible as a grey-blue version of its former self. I climbed into bed and slept the sleep of a happy soul.

The next morning, a pale-yellow Taj greeted me as I stood at my window. Then later as we stood before the monument it was a brilliant white. Neither the guidebook, nor any words could do justice to its beauty and artwork detail. Close up the intricate jeweled friezes are remarkable, delicate as the plants they detail but as ephemeral and timeless, as the love of Shah Jahan for his Mumtaz.

'You could gaze on this building forever and never tire of it,' I announced to my friends. 'Wherever you walk or stand, the Taj is so majestic and beautiful. I think it is the perfect shape, the dome and the minarets are magical.'

'They are more Islamic than Indian. But other aspects of the building are Indian. It is a mix of architecture, but I agree very pleasing to the eye,' Vinni replied.

Like you, I thought. So pleasing to the eye.

The Taj revealed her last mood to us at dawn the next morning. We rose early to view the palace from our balcony. Our balconies were adjoining as our rooms were, so it was perfectly easy to slip out the doors of our rooms, still clad in our pyjamas and meet.

Like a vision from a fairytale, the blue moonlit Taj gradually turned the softest of pinks as the sun rose. The moon by then was a white ghost in the sky now lit with the first rays of the rising sun. It was the sun's turn to dominate the heavens until darkness came again and the moon took centre stage again.

'It's a process that has happened every day since time began, but I have never really appreciated the relay race between the sun and moon before', I said softly.

Vinni looked over at me. His dark eyes glinted with the promise of dawn. Viewing his handsome face in the soft light, I was torn between gazing at him or the distant Taj. They were both beautiful and by now special to me.

I chose Vinni and he chose me. He came close, climbed over the rail of his balcony and joined me at the rail of mine. His strong arm pulled me close, so I stood next to him and touching. My heart raced. I could barely breathe.

'Tanya,' he said. 'You are a special woman, a special person. I would like you in my life, if you would like this too.'

Whatever that meant, whatever it implied future-wise, I did not care. My voice just said, 'Yes, I would like that, Vinni.'

# CHAPTER THIRTY-FIVE

# Purple frogs and Chameleons

We left India. Sashim came with us back to Australia. He would start school in February. Vinni and Vidisha planned a new life for him with them here, but would also make frequent trips to their homeland.

'Our parents are there. They will never leave India. Maybe we will return someday to live there again. But for now, Australia will be our adopted country,' Vinni told me.

'But the cotton mill, your mill, who will run it?'

'We have a manager, a friend of the family. He will be a good manager. I am happier now to work in advertising. That mainly was my focus for the mill. I met with customers. Vidisha did too. She discussed colours and patterns of the textiles. We were both away at a conference when the mill burnt. That is why we are alive and...'

His voice trailed off. The pain in his eyes said it all.

'And Sashim?' Finally, I dared to ask. I knew Sashim had been in the fire. I had seen the burn on his arm.

'Yes, he is lucky. That night, he couldn't sleep because he had been to a birthday party and eaten too many sweets. That always makes him hyperactive. He came downstairs to get a drink and saw the fire already in the factory. He ran back upstairs to wake the workers and the family. His uncle ran from room to room raising the alarm and helping people out. But the fire took hold, and many did not make it out. Sashim did because of my brother-in-law. He made sure Sashim stayed safe outside while he himself continued to help others. My wife…we don't know what happened. Sashim said she was outside safe with him but then she disappeared. We don't know why she went back in.'

'Oh, how terrible, Vinni. I am so sorry for your loss.' I touched his hand as a small gesture of comfort. 'And Vidisha, her children, did she have children?' This question was one I had delayed asking.

'No, Vidisha had no children. She and her husband were unable to have children,' he replied.

I nodded silently. Now I knew the full story or at least the main facts of the tragedy.

Before the start of school term, we took Sashim to the zoo. He loved the otters as Vinni said he would and the Australian animals. Sashim loved all the animals. He never stopped smiling all day.

Vidisha wore a vibrant yellow sari. Her beauty attracted many glances of admiration. Young Sashim seemed to like my company and kept by my side most of the day. Maybe he thought I knew the answers to all his questions. They were interesting questions, showing his intelligence. He, like his aunt, liked colour.

'Are there any pink or purple animals here, Miss Tanya?' he asked.

Unprepared for this unusual question, I pondered a moment before replying, 'Oh, not that I know. But there may be birds and frogs with those colours and the chameleon reptile, it can be any colour, so it matches its environment for camouflage.'

Vidisha, the colour expert, added her expertise. 'Nature uses colour to its advantage. The colour of flowers attracts bees to pollinate the flowers and spread their joy. Colour also helps animals. Some animals use it to attract mates. Like male birds. They are usually prettier than the female. She is often a plain colour to be camouflaged as she sits on the nest. Then other animals use colour to warn others of their poison, so they won't get eaten. Other frogs and insects are green so birds who want to eat them, can't see them in the forest.'

'Really? That is so cool. I want to see the colour changing lizard and the purple, pink frogs too. I like frogs. They are cool and I like green. You have lovely green eyes, Miss Tanya. Why do you have green eyes and we have brown ones? Can we change our colours like the lizard?'

I smiled to thank Sashim for the complement and considered his interesting questions.

'It is how we are born, our eye colour. It comes in our DNA from our parents. You can wear colourful contact lenses to alter your eye colour. Actors do this for movies. People change their colours when they change their clothes. Today your aunt is a beautiful yellow and I am green and white. You are blue and white, and your dad is too.'

'Yes, we like jeans and white shirts. What is DNA?' Sashim spelt it out distinctly savouring each letter.

'It's just how we are. DNA is a code inside us that spells out each part of us, our eye colour, hair colour, size of our nose, how tall we get.'

'I will be tall like my dad and maybe get a big nose too.'

'Yes, you will be tall. Already you are nearly as tall as me!' I laughed.

Sashim drew himself up to full height and measured his height across to my neck.

'Let's find the lizard and the frogs, and after that something to eat. This animal safari makes me hungry,' he exclaimed.

At lunch Sashim sat next to me and our arms touched on the table.

'You are as brown as me, Miss Tanya,' he said.

I smiled and stretched my arm to lay alongside his.

'Yes, I am too. The sun in India, like the sun here, makes me tan a lovely colour. I am as brown as a berry.'

'We match now. We could be family, Miss Tanya. You, me, Dad and Aunt Vidisha.'

I smiled at Sashim and took his hand.

'Yes,' was all I managed to say.

'Tanya is already part of our family', Vinni informed his son.

I smiled up at Vinni and he took my other hand in his. Vidisha smiled her delicious smile from her position opposite.

ℰ

Life continued to surprise, offering its twists and turns. Sean moved in with the park bench lady and ceased to bother me. Our divorce finalised that March and Josie's began with papers signed. Homeless Max nearly became a park bench fixture himself, but Gloria Miller's sister rescued him from such a fate. They met at a MLM conference and rode off into the sunset together chanting 'Executive Gold for us!'

In June, Wisteria Park hosted another romantic wedding. Vinni and I are family now, husband and wife. I can hardly believe it, but it's true. There's a beautiful emerald engagement rock on my finger and a band of gold. My world is a colourful and wonderful place because Colour came to Tangles and brought me happiness.

THE END

# The Last Hotel

Set in a beautiful hideaway on the French Riviera, between the Alpes Maritimes and the shimmering blue Mediterranean, *The Last Hotel* is a heart-warming tale of love and loss and of finding joy in the simplest of pleasures.

It's March 2020, and as flights are cancelled and hotels close in virus-stricken Europe, seven strangers meet by chance. Out of necessity they form a family in lockdown in the last hotel open on the French Riviera.

Young Kaz and Lou have lost their dream jobs in St. Tropez, and Will, a chef from Torquay, is similarly and suddenly unemployed. Jenny came for a holiday with her son, Sasha, but his ballet contract is suspended, and older Australians Maggie and Tim flee Italy. During their stay at the Last Hotel, the new guests meet interesting neighbours, Juliette and Henri, and Deborah, a single mother whose plan for a restful year in Provence is also disrupted.

This improbable gathering of old and young discovers that magic happens when you least expect it. Wars and pestilences can come with no warning out of a cloudless sky, but so too can love take you by surprise. If you believe in magic and serendipity, you will find it here in The Last Hotel.

The novel was inspired by the author's real-life experience of lockdown in 2020.

Now also available as an audiobook.

**Buy Now from joniscottauthor.com or at all good bookstores**

# Whispers Through Time

This historical drama, part true, part fiction, is based on the lives of the author's maternal grandparents, Walter and Winifred, mysterious lives spanning most of the twentieth century.

Encompassing the Boer Wars, the end of the Victorian age and the Titanic tragedy, the characters not only travel onward through these times but also to the colonial outposts of the British Empire.

As the first book of a trilogy, Whispers through Time, introduces the personalities, dreams and motivations of Winifred and her family. The mysteries that surround her life in the past intrigue her real-life grand-daughter, Heady, who tries to unravel them in the present day.

Why did young Winifred leave London alone on a ship to travel to Australia? Why especially in June 1912, just months after the Titanic tragedy?

Where did her brother, Oscar disappear to without a trace? And what happened to her beautiful younger sister, Francesca after her tragic love affair?

Time is an ever-present theme that waxes and wanes like a tide throughout lives.

**Buy Now from joniscottauthor.com or at all good bookstores**

# *Time, Heal my Heart*

In 1914 young husbands and sons set off in high spirits for the grand adventure of war, a war promised to be over by Christmas. Little do they or their loved ones realise that four long years of horror lay ahead.

World War One shatters the peaceful lives of newly wed Australian immigrants, Walter and Winifred. Their families lie over the ocean in England, their brothers fight on the battlefields of Europe. Torn by loyalties, they set off on a perilous sea journey during wartime, shortly after the sinking of the Lusitania by German U boats.

But their neighbour, Lisbette, a girl with a mysterious past, must stay to live in anguish in Australia unable to return to her native France.

The scene shifts from Australia to Gallipoli and the battlefields of Flanders, culminating at the mystical Mont-Saint-Michel off the Normandy coast. Here, Effie, one of many tiny victims of the war, finds refuge in the centuries old monastery.

It is all a matter of time.

Will authorities find Effie's parents at war's end? How long can Winifred's brother, Gustave survive the trenches? And can returning soldiers escape the deadly grip of the Spanish Flu?

Whether read as a stand-alone novel or sequel to *Whispers through Time*, this drama will tear at your heart strings, especially as it is based on a true story.

**Coming Soon. Visit joniscottauthor.com to find out more**